Dedication

*For those with the ability to see what is
hiding in plain sight.
And to those who acknowledge the magic
in the world*

Night at the Legislature

Paranormal Canadiana Collection

Manitoba

Nancy M Bell

Print ISBNs
Amazon print 9780228634010
Ingram Spark 9780228634027
BWL Print 9780228634034

Copyright 2025 by Nancy M Bell
Editor JD Shipton
Cover artist Michelle Lee

Table of Contents

Chapter One

Bother and damn. Elizabeth Warwick glanced out the window of her office at the Manitoba Legislature building. Snow hurled itself against the panes, driven by the demonic wind which confirmed her suspicion that there was a full blown blizzard raging outside. She had better things to do on the night of the Winter Solstice than spend it marooned at work. *Typical Manitoba blizzard. There's a reason they call this place Winterpeg. Buy why tonight, of all nights? It's Winter Solstice and I was planning on spending it with Grandma. Bother and damn.*

Sighing, Elizabeth checked the time. "Oh, my stars! How can it be six-thirty already?" Rising from her desk and pausing to stretch out the kinks in her back, she peered out her office door to be greeted by the sight of empty offices. The third floor looked abandoned. A thread of unease prickled down her spine. She shook her head at what could only have been a passing foolishness. "Now that's just plain silly. With the security in this place, it's not like just any crazies could be lurking about," Elizabeth chided herself. *But where is everyone?* Even Madeline's office was dark, and that woman never left before eight in the evening.

Turning back to her desk, she slid into the chair, minimized the policy document she was working on, and brought up her emails. Earlier, she'd turned off the notifications as the constant interruptions annoyed her when she was working on a time-sensitive project. Cursing herself now, Elizabeth clicked on the message marked Urgent. Her eyes ran briefly over the short paragraph of text. "Well, isn't that just great?" She leaned back in her chair and glanced at the darkened window. "That'll teach me to turn off notifications, won't it?"

Snow beat against the building's storm glass windows, the wind howling and vomiting great gouts of whirling snow that obscured the view to the outside world. The short message still on her screen advised all staff to go home. The forecast was for a prairie blizzard of mammoth proportions. The city expected that all public transportation would be closed down until the storm blew itself out. Elizabeth noted the time the email was sent. Four in the afternoon. Even with her notifications disabled, someone should have come by as they were leaving and let her know. "What was I doing at four?" she muttered. "I haven't left my office since getting coffee around eleven this morning, so why didn't I see everyone leaving?" Casting her mind back over the chaos of her day, the only other time she'd moved was when she visited the washroom. *Maybe that was around four? Surely, I wasn't gone that long? Everyone must have thought I had already gone home.*

Snatching up her phone, she hit Gramma's contact and waited for the phone to ring at the other end. Her grandmother still had a landline, but the chances she would be anywhere but at home in this weather were slim.

"Elizabeth, honey. Where are you?" Gramma's voice hadn't lost its strength or timbre despite her age.

"At work," she replied. "Unfortunately."

"I heard on the news they'd closed all the government buildings, including the Leg and sent everyone home. I've been expecting you for the last three hours. I was getting worried when you didn't answer your phone."

"I didn't hear it. Had the volume turned way down. Sorry. Are the buses still running?"

"Sorry, honey. No. Everything is shut down and they're warning there will most likely be power outages. At least the legislature building has backup generators, you should be okay there."

"Are you going to be okay if that happens? I'm pretty sure your generator should kick in and the stove is gas, so you can still make tea and supper." Elizabeth ran her fingers through her dark blonde hair.

"I'll be just fine. What about you? You're going to be stuck at the Leg until this blows over. I know we planned to celebrate Alban Arthan together, but we'll be together in spirit. Do you have what you need to celebrate?"

Elizabeth laughed. "Well, there's apple juice at the coffee station, I have some granola bars, and I can call up a video with candles on my phone. Lord knows there's holly and mistletoe decorations enough around here, I'm sure I can gather a few sprigs together."

"Do you remember anything about your Great-Grandmother Lizzy? You were named after her, you know. As was I, Liza is a short form of Elizabeth."

"What?" Elizabeth sat up and put her feet flat on the floor. The sudden change of topic put her off balance for a moment. "What does Great-Gramma have to do with our Alban Arthan celebrations?"

"Maybe nothing," Gramma sounded thoughtful, "maybe everything."

"What are you talking about? Are you okay, Gramma? You're not dizzy or feeling disoriented? Should I call your doctor or nine-one-one?"

"I'm fine, silly girl. I'm not losing my marbles just yet. Alban Arthan, Winter Solstice, they're one and the same. You know that. Do you remember your Great-Gramma telling stories about how the veil between this world and the next is thin at certain times of the year? Do you remember any of her stories?"

"Not really. I was pretty young when she passed. I remember her telling me how she worked at the Legislature building in the library when it opened. She told me I would work there one day too. I guess she was right about that."

"That's all you remember? None of the stories she told you?"

Elizabeth searched for her earliest memories of the silver-haired woman who died when Elizabeth was five or six years old. "Something about buffalo and oxen. Oh! And she was always telling me about Medusa and Athena, how Athena was angry with Medusa for being seduced by Poseidon and turned her hair to snakes. Yuck! I still don't understand why she told a little kid that story. Gave me nightmares."

"That's something, at least," Gramma Liza muttered almost too low for Elizabeth to make out the words.

"Gramma. What does all that have to do with anything, right now?"

"Oh, nothing, honey. Just an old lady reminiscing. Now, are you sure you're going to okay all by yourself, or should I call the emergency line and see if someone could come and give you a ride on a snowplow?" Elizabeth could picture the older woman waving her hand dismissively and then craftily changing the subject. There was no point trying to get any more information out of her about the subject of Great-Gramma Lizzy."

"I'll be fine here. I'm more worried about you being alone."

"Oh, I'm not alone. Didn't I mention that? My friend Frank from next door is here. You remember him from the Samhain party at Hallowe'en, don't you?"

Elizabeth smothered an exasperated snort. "You could have mentioned you weren't alone before this. I've been worried like crazy about you being alone in this storm. I've got the news on my computer screen and they're calling this the blizzard of the century. Comparing it to the one in 1947 that shut down the prairies."

"Blizzard of the century. Now that's as apt a comment as I can imagine. Now, if you're sure you're going to be okay, I'm going to let you go. Frank has just come in with mulled wine and honey cakes."

"I'm jealous! Mulled wine and honey cakes trump my apple juice and granola bars. You guys enjoy yourselves and please stay safe. Love you."

"I love you too. Call if you get bored or need anything. Bye honey."

Elizabeth stared at the wallpaper on her phone screen for a long moment. Gramma was acting weird which, she had to admit, was nothing new. But there was something more cryptic than usual behind her words tonight– like she was attempting to convey some hidden message. Elizabeth shook her head and set the phone down. It would take a better mind than hers to even scratch the inner workings of Gramma's mind. The woman might be eighty-five, but she was still sharp as a tack.

The lights flickered and died. Elizabeth held her breath until the generator kicked in and dim light filled the halls. At least she'd have heat, but she'd better see what was left at the coffee station that was still hot. Tucking the phone in her pocket, she hurried down the hall and was relieved to find the light on the coffee maker still shining. Setting a pod in the machine she waited for the coffee to brew. The fridge yielded some yogurt, and meatball sub someone had left. Christmas Eve was only a few days away, and with the storm, it was unlikely the owner of said sandwich would be back for it before its natural expiry She chucked it in the microwave, offered up a silent prayer, and hit the button. The prayer was answered as the machine sprang to life.

Twenty minutes later, stomach full of meatball sub, and a large mug of coffee in hand, Elizabeth made her way back to her office. The sound of high heels on marble stopped her in her tracks. Was there someone else stuck here? The sound echoed through the building; it must be coming from the Pool of the Black Star. It was common knowledge that anything happening in the circular room under the rotunda could be heard throughout the building. Some sort of odd acoustics that no one seemed able to explain. Coffee in hand, Elizabeth hurried toward the marble balustrade that overlooked the eight pointed black star in the centre of the room below.

"Hello? Is somebody there? It's Elizabeth Warwick...Hello?"

There was no response and the sound of the high heels tapping on marble was gone. "I must have imagined it. Most likely all I heard was snow hitting the windows." She cast one last look down at the Black Star and blinked. The dark veining in the marble seemed to flow and move, like blood running from the Star. She blinked again and narrowed her eyes.. The illusion was gone, below her the Black Star lay benignly in the middle of the floor. "Been staring at a computer screen for too long, either that or I'm losing my mind." Suddenly, the familiar building was filled with ominous shadows and the hairs on her arms rose. Heart beating faster than it should, Elizabeth hurried back to the sanctuary of her office, closing and locking the door behind her. She huddled in her chair clutching the comforting warmth of the coffee in her hands. Her mind wasn't on the project she needed to get finished, and at any rate she wasn't willing to trust her work to be saved successfully in the event the generator failed. *No, don't even think that. I'm spooked enough without having to sit in the pitch dark.* Putting the tall back of the chair toward the door, Elizabeth leaned back, kicked off her shoes and pulled her feet up beneath her. Her gaze fastened on the ever changing patterns of the windblown snow as it hammered on the window. She pulled the large wool shawl she kept in her office around her and snuggled into the warmth.

There were voices in the wind, she was sure of it. Great-Gramma Lizzy used to say that. What a funny thing to remember after all this time. It must be because Gramma was talking about her earlier.

Chapter Two

"Elizabeth. Elizabeth. Wake up, child."

Someone was gently shaking her. Elizabeth sank deeper into the chair, pulling the shawl closer.

"Elizabeth, wake up. You must wake up."

The voice was insistent, and it intruded on the lovely dream she was having. She twisted away from whoever it was that was disturbing her. *Wait! The building is empty, there's no one here but me.* The unsettling thought banished the last wisps of the dream. Cautiously, she cracked open one eye, just a slit. Without a doubt, there was a shadowy figure by her chair. Elizabeth shot to her feet, throwing the shawl aside and grabbed for the old umbrella sticking out of its stand– a relic left by the former occupant of her office.

"Who are you?" Her voice wavered in spite of her best efforts.

"Calm down, child. I mean you no harm." The woman stepped into the dim light coming into the office from the emergency lights in the corridor.

Elizabeth blinked. The woman seemed harmless enough, though her clothing was odd. Like something from the 1920's. A dark fitted jacket skimmed her hips above a narrow, straight skirt that fell just below the knees. Under the jacket, the silky folds of a scarf accented the crisp pale yellow blouse that peeked out of the unbuttoned jacket. She looked familiar somehow, but that was impossible. Elizabeth knew everyone who worked at the Legislature, and this person wasn't someone she recognized.

"Who are you?" She raised the umbrella a bit higher, hoping her trembling hands didn't betray her frantic fear.

"I mean you no harm. Put that silly umbrella back where it belongs and come with me. I have much to tell you and we have very little time."

"What do you mean? Tell me what and time for what? It's not like we can go anywhere in this weather, we're both stuck here until it quits." Bewildered, Elizabeth shook her head. *Maybe I'm still dreaming. That must be it. I need to wake up.*

Thunder rolled through the storm, drowning out the wind for a moment, and was followed almost directly by a blinding flash of lightning. Elizabeth whirled toward the window, heart shuddering in her chest. How could it be thundering in the depths of December? The umbrella was plucked from her fingers and tossed back into the stand. Heart still pulsing in her throat, she turned back to the odd woman.

"Come with me. You must, so I can prepare you for what is to take place this night." The woman held out her hand.

"Who are you? I'm not going anywhere until you tell who you are and how you are here when I know the building is empty." Elizabeth stood her ground.

"My name is Elizabeth, but you may call me Lizzy. And why I am here is simple. I work here. In the library." She stepped forward and grasped Elizabeth's hand. "Come along, we need to hurry."

"Work here?" She allowed herself to be towed out of her office and down the corridor. The woman's hand felt solid enough, but unsettling sensations rippled up Elizabeth's arm.

"You can't work here. I would know you, if you did. And we don't have a library...well we did...but now it's the reading room..."

"Yes, yes. The reading room, if you like. Now hurry." Lizzy broke into a jog, forcing Elizabeth to keep up.

Elizabeth trotted along behind Lizzy, head still whirling with unanswered questions. There was something odd about the reading room, she remembered Tom, the night watchman, telling her stories. He'd told her he'd seen a woman in old fashioned clothing in the room replacing books on shelves and sorting through folders. Yes, it was all coming back now. How when Tom called out to her, the woman had on one occasion ignored him and somehow disappeared before he could reach her. And how on another night, she'd looked up in surprise, clutched the folders to her chest and simply vanished before his eyes. Adrenaline jolted through Elizabeth's body, her breath catching in her throat. She stopped dead in her tracks, pulling the other woman to a halt.

"Who are you? You tell me right now or I'm not budging from this spot," Eliabeth ground the words out between clenched teeth. Clenched, she acknowledged, to keep them from chattering.

"There's no time, child. Come." Lizzy tugged on her hand. "I promise I'll explain everything once we reach the library." She glanced upward as another roll of thunder shook the building. "We must hurry. The time draws near. So dramatic, what with thunder in middle of winter." Now she sounded worried and scared.

"What are you afraid of and why won't you tell me who you are?" Elizabeth refused to move another step until she had some answers.

"You are a most stubborn and obstinate child. Do you realize that?" Lizzy glared at her.

"Yup, that's me. Mom says I take after my great-grandmother." Elizabeth nodded.

Lizzy shook her head and muttered something under her breath. After another glance upward, she stepped closer to the younger woman. "I told you my name is

Lizzy. What I haven't told you is that we have met before, although you were probably too young to remember." She paused and took a deep breath. "I am your Great Grandmother Lizzy. There I've told you what you wanted to know, now come, we need to hurry if we are to be on time."

Dumbfounded, Elizabeth allowed herself to be herded to the second floor and into the reading room. In the dim light, it looked different. The tall room was still lined with sky high shelves of leatherbound books, the same balconies ran around the edges of the room, but it was different. Older somehow, and the furniture was in different places. Lizzy, wait, *Great Gramma* Lizzy pushed her down into a padded armchair and took the one opposite her.

"You can't be Great Gramma Lizzy. She died when I was just a kid. Why are you lying to me?" Elizabeth pushed on the arms of the chair but found she couldn't stand up.

"Do you recall your grandmother telling you that in every generation of the Warwick family there will always be one girl child named Elizabeth?"

She nodded. "Gramma said it was a family tradition that went back a hundred years or more. Back to when our family first settled here. But what's that got to do with you claiming to be my dead great grandmother?"

"Ah, it has everything to do with it, lovey. Now, if you don't believe me, why don't you call your grandmother and ask her to send you a photo of your Great Grandmother Lizzy? I know there's one in the old family album that is kept beside the family bible. That should clear things up and then I can get on with explaining why I'm here, and more importantly, why you are here. Go on, call her." Lizzy sat back in her chair and folded her hands in her lap.

Elizabeth fished her phone out of her pocket and called her grandmother. She answered on the first ring.

"Elizabeth, how are things going there?"

"Weird, that's how things are going. There's a woman here who is claiming to be my great grandmother, and she wants me to ask you to send a picture of a photo that is in the old album by the bible."

"Oh, what a good idea! I can do that. Hold on a second." The line went silent.

"Gramma?" Elizabeth held the phone away from her ear. "Did I just drop the call?"

"No, no. I'm here, just getting the album down. Frank is going to take the picture and send it to you so I can stay on the line with you. You know how technically challenged I can be. There, you should have it in a minute."

Elizabeth's phone lit up with a notification that she had a text. "Hang on, let me take a look." She flipped to her texts and brought up the image. For a second she forgot to breathe. The woman in the photo was a dead ringer for the woman sitting across from her. Even down to the fact she was wearing the same clothing.

"Gramma, how can this be? This person here with me is a dead ringer for Great Gramma Lizzy. Is this some kind of joke? Or am I still dreaming. If I am, I want to wake up, like right now."

"Breathe, Elizabeth. Just breathe for a moment. That's a good girl. Now listen to me. Have I ever lied to you?"

"No." The words were barely a whisper.

"And I'm not lying now. The person with you is indeed your great grandmother. So of course she is a dead ringer, as you said, for the woman in the photo." She paused. "Dead being the operative word."

"I'm sitting here with a ghost?" Elizabeth's voice was flat, incredulous.

"Not exactly, dear. Lizzy is my mother, and your great grandmother. More importantly, she is also the Guardian. That is why she is there in the library of the legislature building. She waits, and she guards, until such time as she is needed, and until another comes to take her place. I'm sure she can explain things much better than I can. Good luck, my darling. I will see you tomorrow."

The phone went blank in Elizabeth's hand. She turned stunned eyes to the woman sitting calmly opposite her.

"What exactly is it that you are guarding against?" Elizabeth decided she must surely be having a *very* lucid dream, and she might as well go along with it. Maybe it was the sub sandwich from the break room?

"That's a more sensible attitude, love. I can't imagine a child of my bloodline being anything other than wise enough to know the truth when she hears it. I am the Guardian of the secrets of this building. The secrets hidden in plain sight. I will explain those later, or Septimus will. What you need to know now is that I am The Guardian, *The* Elizabeth. This is why there must be a girl child named Elizabeth in each generation. Once every hundred years the sanctity of this building is threatened, and there must be The Elizabeth present to assist in nullifying that threat. I fulfilled my duty one hundred years ago this night. Now it is your turn. For you are the next Guardian."

Chapter Three

Elizabeth shot to her feet. "Whoa! Whoa! Go back and ride down that trail again." She held up both hands palm outward. "First off, my great grandmother is dead, so you can't possibly be her. Secondly, I'm just plain old me, Elizabeth. Not *The* Elizabeth, whatever that's supposed to mean."

Lizzy folded her hands in her lap in a serene pose. "Sit down, Elizabeth. I know this all seems impossible, and I do wish you could have been given a bit of preparation beforehand, but... Well, we play with the hand that is dealt us. Sit down, please."

Against her better judgment, Elizabeth subsided into the chair. What kind of crazy dream was this? And why couldn't she wake up? She pinched her arm hard, wincing at the sharp burst of pain. *Nope, still dreaming.* "What do you mean prepare me? Prepare me for what?" *Might as well play along with the crazy ghost lady.*

"Let me start at the beginning. The land the legislature sits on has always been sacred, hallowed if you like. It is close to the conjunction of the two great rivers, the Red and the Assiniboine, powerful conductors of energies. The energies that flow through the earth, picture them like the blood vessels of Mother Earth if that makes it easier to envision."

"You mean like ley lines?" Elizabeth interrupted her.

"Ah, I see you are aware of some things. The energies are related to ley lines only in the way that ley lines are the straight alignments of sites of concentrated energies. The actual earth energies weave through the planet, some describe the two energies as male and female, some as positive and negative, what is important is that they are opposites that complement each other. They balance each other, if you will."

"You're talking about the same kind of energy lines that Hamish Miller dowsed through southwest England. From Cornwall to East Anglia?" Elizabeth leaned forward; her curiosity piqued. "He called them the Michael and Mary lines."

"Exactly so. Those energy lines exist all over the planet." Lizzy nodded.

"Wait, you're saying that the legislature building is sitting on one of those lines?"

"Not just one of those lines, but a node. A place where the two lines meet and the energy gathers, before travelling on. Some call them vortexes, or vortices. What you need to understand is that the two energies must balance each other. Over the course of a hundred years the male energy surges and reaches its peak. That is where we come in, The Elizabeths."

"Uh uh. I'm playing along with you because I can't seem to wake up, but I'm not one of The Elizabeths—"

"Hush and listen to me." Lizzy fixed her with a stern gaze. "We are Warwicks, whether through maternal or paternal lineage. It was a Warwick who set the safeguards in place when the building was erected. Their blood flows in both our veins. You will have a daughter called Elizabeth one day, and she will have a daughter named Elizabeth. We are The Guardians."

"You mean all these Elizabeths will be stuck here in the legislature building forever?" Elizabeth's head was spinning, a cold shiver of horror running down her spine.

"No dear." Lizzy chuckled. "There is only one Guardian at a time. Each Elizabeth will do her part to maintain the balance, then she goes on to live a full life until she is ready to pass into the next realm, then she relieves the current Guardian of her duty. I am the first and current Guardian of our line, and I prefer to linger here in the library where I worked when I was young. When it is your turn, you can choose to linger wherever you like within the building."

"What if I don't want *a turn*? What if I refuse to go along with this nonsense?"

"That would be your choice, of course. The result will be that the male energies continue to grow, to weaken the feminine. The male energies would take precedence in the world of man, much like it was in the 1800s and early 1900s when women were chattels, had no vote, and owned nothing, not even the right to control their bodies or their destinies."

"You mean when we couldn't go out without wearing a hat and gloves and accompanied by a chaperone, or decide who we wanted to marry?" Elizabeth remembered her history lessons about the suffragettes.

"Correct. This is why it is so important to maintain the balance of the energies. Too much of either isn't healthy for the state of world." Lizzy nodded.

"But, if what you say is true...this is only a tiny part of the whole world. What difference can it make either way?"

"A whole unit is made up of many tiny parts. Each tiny part is as important as the next, indeed as important as the whole unit. When each tiny part fulfils its task, then it strengthens the whole. We only have control of our tiny part, but you must never forget how important that tiny part is." Lizzy leaned over and grasped Elizabeth's hands in hers. "Are things starting to make sense now?"

"Sort of." In spite of herself, Elizabeth found herself nodding.

"Good, then." Lizzy patted her hands and sat back.

"Why is the legislature building so important to this though?"

"Think on it, child. Where are the laws of the land created, where are decisions that affect thousands made? Here in this building. The architects of this structure understood the energies that flow here. They created the building using sacred geometry in a manner to encourage its inhabitants to be better people, more moral, more intelligent. In the Middle Ages they believed sacred geometry could recreate the divine. Once you meet Septimus, he can explain much better than I the symbolism that exists within these walls. Secrets hidden in plain sight." Lizzy's eyes lost focus and a brilliant smile creased her face. "Oh, I remember my astonishment and joy when they were revealed to me." She blinked and refocused on Elizabeth. "One thing I can tell you, open your mind and remember that the sphinx looks both east and west. To the sunrise and the sunset. The beginning of the day and the end. Then the path of the moon and stars across the heavens."

"Are you trying to tell me that whoever this architect was, that he thought the blueprint of the building could make ordinary Manitobans into better people? Like a higher order or something?" Elizabeth couldn't quite come to terms with the fact that a clearly well educated, intelligent man who understood the principles of engineering could believe that his design could encourage people to become more enlightened. The reference to the sphinx was lost in her consideration of the architect's supposed goal.

"That is exactly what he believed. And for our sakes, let us hope he is correct." Lizzy got to her feet. "Come along, now. I believe Septimus is waiting."

"Septimus. You keep mentioning him, but I know there's no one else in the building." She glanced at the snow covered window where the blizzard still howled.

"And yet, I am here with you. Come along. We need to go to the rotunda to meet him." Lizzy held out her hand.

"In for a penny, in for a pound," Elizabeth muttered, quoting something her mother used to say. She took Lizzy's hand, suppressing a slight shiver, and let herself be pulled to her feet. "Why the rotunda?"

"That is something you must see for yourself." Lizzy smiled and led the way out of the library.

Chapter Four

Elizabeth followed the other woman through the corridor and up to the rotunda. She was glad of the guiding hand as her head was awhirl with confusion and questions that had no answers. How could this woman, this self-proclaimed ghost, be Great Grandmother Lizzy? And if she was, then perhaps everything she said in the library was true and Elizabeth was doomed to lurk around in the stupid building until the next Elizabeth, or Guardian, or whatever she was supposed to be, showed up. Like a hundred years from now? *You have got to be kidding me! I really, really need to wake up.*

"Hurry along now. Quit dawdling, dear," Lizzy's voice cut into Elizabeth's jumbled thoughts.

Resigning herself to the possibility that she might not be dreaming, Elizabeth allowed the woman to draw her up the wide flight of steps flanked by the two enormous bison statues. She stumbled for a moment, there was movement caught out of the corner of her eye. Elizabeth could swear that one of the bison turned its head and looked at her. But somehow it had taken on the aspect of a bull. Shaking her head, she responded to the tug of Lizzy's hand and hurried her steps.

They reached the top of the last flight of stairs and stepped onto the polished floor outside the arch that led into the rotunda. The marble balustrade in the centre of the room glimmered in the dim light, most of the luminance lost in the soaring dome above the round opening inside the railing.

"Ah, good. We are in plenty of time." Great Gramma Lizzy stepped into the room.

"Time for what?" Elizabeth whispered. The rotunda and the corresponding room below it always made her want to whisper. It was a well-known fact that anything someone said in the lower room echoed back to them and often voices and sounds from other parts of the building could be heard there.

"Come along, we'll wait by the balustrade." Lizzy walked across the tiled pattern laid into the floor.

Elizabeth followed her, laying a hand on the railing when she stopped beside her spectral ancestor. She glanced down at the eight-pointed black star embedded in the floor directly beneath the opening above and also directly under the dome that soared overhead and upheld the famous golden statue that graced the roof of the building. She glanced upward toward the pale blue and gold that decorated the dome.

"He isn't The Golden Boy, you know," Lizzy spoke softly.

"No? Isn't that what everyone calls that statue?" She leaned on the rail with one hip and regarded the older woman, even though she looked no older than Elizabeth herself.

"That's true. But his real name is Eternal Youth. This building was created in the image of a temple, King Soloman's Temple to be exact."

"Really? I've never heard that."

"Were you aware that the creator of the blueprints for the building was a mason? And so, there is masonic symbolism all through this building." Lizzy met Elizabeth's gaze.

"No, I wasn't aware of that. It kind of explains some of the things that seem out of place in a provincial legislature building." Elizabeth let her gaze wander over the elaborate rosettes on the walls and the globe lights surrounding the room. She turned and glanced back through the arch into the Grand Staircase Hall with its bison, which actually seemed to belong, but the topflight of steps was flanked by two women's heads, one on each side of the hall which was just plain weird. Not to mention the ox heads adorning the walls, eight of them to be exact. Maybe they were supposed to represent the oxen from the Red River carts of the Métis?

"Yes, it explains much and leaves much to be explained," Lizzy's reply was enigmatic to say the least.

"Okay, but what does that have to do with me, or you for that matter?"

Lizzy glanced over her shoulder, as if expecting someone to be there, then turned back with a resigned sigh. "Do you know the story of Hiram Abiff? It is what many of the rituals of the Masons are based on. And it has everything to do with what is going on here this night."

"Hiram Abiff? I can't say that I know that story. How does something that happened eons ago have anything to do with the here and now?"

"Oh, I do wish Septimus would hurry up and get here," Lizzy fretted. "But never mind, I can fill you in on Hiram Abiff and then it should be clear how the two are connected."

"What two? The Masons and Hiram or Hiram and whatever crazy thing is supposed to be happening here." *I really, really need to wake up. Now! This is the weirdest dream I've ever had.*

"Both of those things, dear child. Hear me out and I will try to answer your questions when you have heard the whole story. Hiram Abiff was a very talented artificer who was sent by the King of Tyre to King Solomon so he could execute the principal works in the interior of what would become King Solomon's Temple. He was considered a Master.

According to the legend I am aware of, after the Temple was completed, one day Hiram was engaged in communion with the Grand Architect of the Universe, whom we refer to as God, in the Holy of Holies. He was approached by three men, fellow worshipers but of a lower standing. These three men were Jubela, Jubelo and Jubelum. They asked for the *Master's Word,* which is the secret name of God. That name is known only to those who have achieved the highest degree in the Masonic order. When Hiram refused to reveal the sacred name to the men, they became enraged. The first man to strike a blow, again according to legend, was Jebela. This man hit Hiram across the throat with a 24 inch gauge. This is the compass with two points that you see today in many Masonic symbols. The second man to attack Hiram was Jubelo, he hit Hiram in the left breast with a metal square. Another symbol you see in Masonic icons. The remaining man, Jubelum struck Hiram in the forehead with a gavel. The mortally injured man fell to the ground and died at the feet of his attackers. His blood was shed within the sacred precincts of the temple. Realizing they had murdered a man of the High and Sublime Degree, the men smuggled the body, under cover of darkness, out of the East Gate of the Temple and buried him on Mount Moriah."

"That's a horrible story," Elizabeth broke into the narrative, hugging her arms around her waist and hunching her shoulders, as if against a winter chill.

"It is, I agree. But let me finish. The next morning King Solomon showed up to see how work was progressing and found all the workers milling around as there was no one to give them the plans for the day's work. When a search turned up no sign of Hiram Abiff, King Solomon became worried and sent out twelve Fellowcraft Masons to search for any sign of the man. King Solomon himself decided to go with the three men who searched to the East of the temple. They found a sprig of the acacia tree which should not have been where it was and so discovered the burial place. The three men and the king dug up the body and a search was made for the *Master's Word*, the Name of God, but all they could find was the letter G. The *Master's Word* was lost. King Solomon lamented the loss, and attempts were made to resurrect Hiram. First they took up Hiram's body using the Boaz grip, which is the handshake grip used by First Degree Masons to identify themselves. When this proved unsuccessful, they moved on to the Jachin grip, which is the handshake grip used by Second Degree Masons to identify themselves. This also proved to be unsuccessful. Then Solomon took over from the first three men. He took Hiram in the Third Degree grip of the Master Mason, which employed the five points of fellowship, and then spoke into Hiram's ear the phrase *Ma Ha Bone*. The man took a deep breath and opened his eyes. The king was much relieved his architect was back among the living. While Hiram appeared to be resurrected, he was never the same and hid himself away in seclusion. King Solomon had the three murderers hunted down and each was killed according to the blow he had delivered to the murdered man. So Jubela had his throat cut, Jubulo was stabbed in the left breast with the edge of a metal square, and Jubelum was hit on the head with a gavel or mallet. So, each man died by the method he used in the murder of Hiram Abiff."

"Okay, weird and gruesome, but I still don't really see what that has to do with me." Elizabeth averted her eyes from the Black Star below as it seemed to swim in her gaze.

"Hiram Abiff eventually died an angry man. When this building was built, it was with a wish to seek and keep the balance between light and darkness. Good and Evil, if you wish. Hiram's spirit morphed into something else entirely; no longer human and a servant of the Dark. I'm not clear on how, or why, that spirit became attached to this building, but I assure you it is. It may be because this building was constructed so accurately to mirror King Solomon's Temple."

"You expect me to believe that this Hiram person is here?"

"No, not exactly. Not the person who was murdered so long ago. But an aspect of his anger and feelings of betrayal that have become what will manifest itself here this night of the longest dark."

"The Elizabeth, I greet you," an unfamiliar voice came out of the shadows.

"Oh my God!" Elizabeth whirled around toward the sound.

"No, I am not a god. And I greet you as well, newfound The Elizabeth."

"Septimus, you have no idea how glad I am to see you." Lizzy drew the figure in a dark, old fashioned suit and top hat into the glow of the emergency lights.

"And I you." He bent and pressed a kiss to Lizzy's cheek. "I see you have already started to enlighten your great granddaughter about the task at hand."

Elizabeth snorted. "I'm not sure how *enlightened* I am, or how much I'm buying into this crazy story."

"That is to be expected. I would be disappointed if you accepted the things we are telling you as whole cloth. It is good to question, but please keep an open mind."

"Shall I leave you now?" Lizzy asked, glancing toward Elizabeth.

"No!" Elizabeth cried.

"Yes, of course. You will know when you are needed later," Septimus replied at the same time as Elizabeth's denial. He bowed to Lizzy.

"Until later." She tipped her head and then disappeared through the arched doorway into the Grand Staircase Hall, the sound of her high heels clicking on the tiles echoed in the rotunda long after she was gone.

Chapter Five

"I'm pleased to make your acquaintance, Miss Elizabeth. I am Septimus." He bowed over her hand which she reluctantly allowed him to take in his own. He felt as solid as the librarian, but there was no way he could be real.

"What, no *The* Elizabeth?" She knew she sounded petulant, but she was far from happy with the whole affair.

A smile lit up the man's face. "No, not yet. You won't really be The Elizabeth until the task is completed. And even then, you will not take your place here as The Guardian until your time has come. Let us not worry about that at the moment. There are things I need to tell you and show you. Come." Septimus gestured toward the archway into the Grand Staircase Hall.

"Sure, why not." Elizabeth shrugged and moved in that direction. "Like Alice in Wonderland, this just keeps getting more curiouser and curiouser." She stopped beside the tall man in the shadow of the arch. The bison statues seemed to shimmer and waver, as if she was looking at them through a heat haze. One moment they were the familiar bison and the next they were somehow huge bulls. Elizabeth shook her head and blinked. *Nope, same thing. Damn.* "What is going on?" she demanded of the man beside her.

"It begins. But there is still time to explain how we must proceed." He led the way toward the top of the first flight of broad stairs. First, do you know anything about the layout of a temple, not necessarily Solomon's, but temples in general?"

Elizabeth shook her head. "I can't say that I do. Why, is it important?"

"It is. So let me begin at the beginning. A temple is comprised of many parts all incorporated into one building. The first is the Room of Protection which is where we are standing now."

"Protection? Protection from what?"

"From evil, from immoral thought and deed. The subliminal message of this area is that you are entering sacred ground. The Bison, while being an important part of Manitoba's history, also stand in the place of the bulls that traditionally guarded temple entrances."

"What temple entrances? Like churches?" Elizabeth frowned.

"No, no, dear." He chuckled a little. "Ancient Egypt is the motherland of all magic, and that is what you will find here in this building. Come." He took her hand and led her toward the top step of the uppermost staircase.

"Okay." She stood at his side, carefully not looking at the shimmering bison.

"Now, what do you see at the south entrance to the hall?"

"There's a weird woman's head in the stone at the top of the arch. Why is that important?"

"Ah, that is not just any woman, that is Medusa—"

"Medusa? What is a Greek goddess doing here?" Elizabeth interrupted him.

"She is an apotropaic figure. She has the power to send evil away and Medusa is the embodiment of apotropaic power. Now look over at the north entrance." Septimus turned her toward that direction. "What do you see there?"

"Another face in the keystone? Who is that supposed to be?"

"That is Athena, goddess of war. She is the embodiment of democracy and protector of cities. The two balance each other. Their message is that no one with evil or selfish intent should enter here. They encourage knowledge and intelligence mixed with morality and upholding democracy."

"Sure, I guess..."

"Not convinced yet, are you? That's good, my dear." He patted her arm. "It is good to ask questions and not take everything at face value. I only ask you to keep an open mind. Now, notice the lion heads that are on the walls. Lions are associated with the sun gods, and they are also symbolic guardians. In Egyptian myth, they guard temples and palaces, the rising and setting sun, and the gateway to the underworld. There are fourteen of them here. There are also eight oxen skulls. They represent the bukrama, which is what the heads of the sacrificial oxen were called once the Druid priest hung them over the altar during a ritual. Bukrama deflect evil. The gargoyles you see are also to ward off evil spirits."

"What does all this have to do with the Manitoba Legislature, for heaven's sake?" Elizabeth was still trying to wrap her head around the fact she'd walked through this hall every day and never noticed what was right in front of her nose. If someone had asked her if Medusa and Athena, or stone lion heads for that matter, were in the building, she would have said no. And thought the person was odd for asking such a thing.

"The man who designed the building was a Mason of a high degree. He incorporated many things into his design in order to ensure that corruption was kept out of the legislature. So that is why this Grand Staircase Hall is the Room of Protection."

"What's going on with the bison? Why are they shimmering and flickering between bison and bull?" She took a quick look, and the images swam before her eyes. She blinked and looked away to ward off the dizziness that swept through her.

"It is because this is the night of the Winter Solstice–the longest night. This is the night that The Abiff arises to try and upset the balance of light and dark. It is the aspect of Hiram Abiff that is bent on vengeance for the manner of his death and unwanted resurrection. For the rest of his natural life, he dwelt with one foot in our world and one in the realm of the dead. All the spirit knows is hate, and cloaks himself in darkness. We are the light, and we will not let that happen. The protectors that you see around us that have hidden in plain sight will also rise up and assist us. When the time is come, The Elizabeth will come into the Hall, and they will awaken at her call."

"The Elizabeth? You mean Gramma Lizzy...or me?" Elizabeth swallowed and clenched her hands. This was so not what she had planned for this evening.

"Tonight, you are The Elizabeth. Lizzy did her part one hundred years ago this night. She is here to support you and help guide you if we should become separated. And she will guard us during the final element of the ritual."

"What am I supposed to do? I have no idea about any of this..."

"You are a Warwick. When the time comes you will know, it is in your bloodline. Never fear, child. You won't be alone. Now a few more things about this Hall before we proceed. As we go, you will notice there are numbers that are repeated throughout the building. Take for instance these stairs. There are three flights of thirteen steps each. They are enclosed by four walls. The architect called it the Grand Staircase Hall, but it is actually a perfect square. It measures sixty-six-point-six feet on each side.”

“Wait a minute! Isn’t six-six-six supposed to be the number of the beast in Revelations?”

“That is what the Bible says, yes. But Six-six-six is referenced in *De Occulata Philosophia* and in that text six-six-six is assigned to the sun which rules over all gods, heaven and earth. So, you can see perhaps why it is employed in this area, yes?”

“I suppose...” Elizabeth struggled to wrap her head around all the information Septimus was proffering.

“Now, we move into the Sanctuary. The second part of a temple. Here, in this building, it is this room at the top of the stairs and situated in front of the doors to the Legislature Chambers.” He walked forward under the arched doorway and waited for Elizabeth to join him in the circular room. It was eerily quiet, as if the room was holding its breath and waiting for them.

“This is, in effect, The Altar.” He gestured toward the marble balustrade that allowed a person to look directly down into the room below where an eight-pointed black star was inlaid in the marble floor. “We are directly under the dome which holds the statue of Eternal Youth. The one most people refer to as The Golden Boy, but which the architect called by the name of Eternal Youth and in fact represents Hermes. Now that in itself is interesting as there are actually three Hermes. First, going back to ancient Egypt, he is associated with Thoth who had the body of a man and the head of a hawk, then in Roman mythology Hermes is associated with Mercury, and finally, he is Hermes Trismegithus. But that isn't important right now. I apologize for getting sidetracked. This area is bounded by the balustrade which guards the round opening down to the next floor and is the hub of everything that is to occur this night. Notice the design of the tiles on the floor: It is a geometric wheel with a tessellated border. The Greek Key which represents the eternal quest for knowledge. Now look over the balustrade."

Elizabeth moved forward and peered over the marble railing, gripping the top of it as the eight-pointed black star set into the tiles below swam into view. "I see the black star." She looked up at Septimus wondering what was so significant about it.

"Yes, the black star. It is perfectly centred under the dome and therefore also directly under the golden statue on the roof. The star is a representation of the pole star, Polaris, or you might know it as the North Star. This is the stage on which the movements of the cosmos play out. The star below us is the actual Altar. If you notice the dark veining in the marble surrounding the star, it represents the blood of the sacrificial offering.

"Whoa, hold on there. What blood and what sacrifice? If you for one minute think I'm going to allow you or anyone else to sacrifice me..." Elizabeth pulled away from Septimus and backed up toward the entrance to the Hall.

"Peace, child. No one is sacrificing anyone. Tonight, or any night. Come, while we still have some time, let me show you something interesting about the building. Much of it is comprised of what is termed Sacred Geometry. Sacred Geometry is about balance. It is what allowed those masons of long ago to erect those huge cathedrals and temples and have them stand and not fall into themselves for lack of support. Sacred Geometry is believed to be the key to the mind of God and allow mankind to recreate the divine. This building is built to deliver a divine, subliminal message, to impel people toward faith, hope, morality and charity. Sacred Geometry is based on the Golden Rule or the Golden Section, which is the divine proportion resulting in esthetically pleasing forms in nature. Like a flower's petals, or a nautilus shell which has been bisected."

"I guess I can see that, in a way. Like some musical compositions are more soothing than others," Elizabeth mused, intrigued in spite of her misgivings about this whole affair.

Now, the numbers are fascinating. There is a repetition of certain numbers and ratios everywhere if you know how to see them. Five and Eight are fairly prominent. There are five archways on each side of the Grand Staircase, on the panels above are five gold rosettes. There are eight Corinthian columns in the rotunda, mirrored by eight Doric columns in the Portico below. The black star has eight points, there are eight lamps surrounding the black star. The Rosettes in the Grand Staircase have five or eight petals. The staircase is thirteen feet across, and there are three flights of steps with thirteen stairs in each flight. Here," he waved toward the balustrade, "the area across the opening is thirteen feet, the arched door leading into the Legislature Chambers has thirteen circular moldings around the door. There are thirteen lights down each corridor in the building, there are thirteen media chairs behind the Speaker's Chair. So, we see five, eight and thirteen. Five plus eight equals thirteen, and they are part of the Fibonacci sequence of numbers which mirrors the Golden Section."

A huge peal of thunder shook the building, and the lights flickered. Septimus glanced toward the rotunda and moved toward the balustrade. Elizabeth followed him, eyes drawn to the odd lights dancing and twisting upward from the portico below.

"What is happening?" she whispered.

"It is beginning. The thunder is The Abiff's anger made manifest in our realm. Come, we must awaken the protectors." Septimus spared the weird lights swirling over the black star and up through the balustrade a backward glance and then hurried toward the top of the Grand Staircase. "Come, hurry."

"But I don't know what I'm supposed to do," Elizabeth muttered. "This is insanity. Whoever heard of thunder in a blizzard?" She moved to stand beside the tall man and gazed down the wide staircase. Thunder roared again and the marble under her feet trembled. She swallowed hard to keep from losing the little that was in her stomach. Was it really thunder or was it the Abiff spirit's voice? "What am I supposed to do?" she beseeched Septimus. "How am I supposed to make stone statues walk or wake up or whatever it is you're expecting them to do?"

"For heaven's sake, girl. It's in your blood. Open your mind and let it flow." The voice at her side was deep and husky.

Elizabeth choked back a yelp and turned toward the person who had appeared seemingly out of nowhere. "Who...who are you," she managed to get out before she recognized the features. "Oh, no, no, this can't be happening."

"I'm Athena, goddess of war and all that. Will you get on with it, girl. Time's a'wasting."

"But...but, you're just a stone head up on the arch..." Elizabeth tore her gaze from the woman's face and sure enough the keystone was missing its stone face. "Oh, God. Oh, God."

"Now's not the time for prayer, although if you don't get on with it, prayer might be all we have left." The voice came from her other side, just behind her shoulder.

Holding her breath, Elizabeth ventured a quick peek and jumped forward with a squeak.

"What's the matter with you? Never seen a head of snakes before?" Medusa laughed. "Better get used to it. It's going to be a long night. And we have evil to defeat. Nothing like a good war once in a while, eh Athena?"

Elizabeth turned to Septimus. "What should I do. How do I start?" She focused on the crazy man, her eyes wide and threatening mania. It was better than the two impossible women behind her. *Snakes!* Her skin crawled.

He put his hands on her shoulders and looked into her eyes. "You two shush," he admonished the two goddesses. Then, turned his full attention to Elizabeth. "Calm your breathing, calm your heart. Deep breaths. Feel the earth under your feet, down through the marble, through the concrete down into the heart of the earth. Feel the connection, let it flow up through your feet into your body. Breathe in the golden light, it's warm and it is comfort." He waited.

Elizabeth tried to do what he asked. At first she couldn't control the galloping of her heart, but after a moment of deep breathing, she felt it slow. Then, even though she felt silly, she listened to his voice and allowed her attention to flow downward. She jolted with astonishment when the earth answered her, acknowledged her spirit, and flooded her with warmth and light. She closed her eyes to savour the feeling and marvelled at the golden and warm brown and russet lights wavering on the inside of her eyelids.

"Now, open yourself to the heavens. Let your spirit fly high, find the heaven star, find the bright light and let it flow down through you. Keep your eyes closed if that makes it easier, then allow the two energies to flow around you. Merged, but still separate. When you feel ready, open your eyes and follow your instincts. Don't think, just act."

Elizabeth reached upward and was rewarded with a spark of purest light that grew and brightened as it descended down and into her body, or maybe her spirit, she wasn't sure and didn't think it mattered. Don't think, act, she told herself. The lights flowed and crackled around her, the power building like static on her skin. When it began to itch, she opened her eyes and threw out her arms toward the Hall which was now bathed in swirling light, almost as if the northern lights were flowing through the air. Elizabeth saw her body standing at the top of the stairs, bathed in brilliant light, as if her spirit was somehow separate from her body—but not in a bad way. Energy and joy wrapped around her. She threw her spirit back at her corporeal body and suddenly knew exactly what she needed to do.

"Awake! The time is near. Prepare for battle. Prepare to protect what we hold most dear. I am The Elizabeth and I call you to come to my aid in this time of peril. Awake guardians! Awake protectors! Awake and do your duty!"

She blinked and came back to herself. Elizabeth shook her head and looked down at her body. It seemed that tiny lights still shimmered over her skin leaving trails of light when she moved her hands.

"That was well done, indeed," Athena remarked before she strode off down one of the hallways.

"Not bad, I have to say," Medusa said staring after Athena, the snakes coiling around her head. "We'll take the basement to start, just in case something comes in there once The Abiff shows up. I have to say I could use some excitement after a hundred years of staring at some of the idiots that come through here." Without another word she stalked off down the opposite hallway to the one Athena took.

A lazy roar drew Elizabeth's attention to the lion heads, they were sprouting necks and chests and front legs as she watched.

"Holy cow," she whispered. "I can't believe I'm seeing this."

Chapter Six

"Believe it, for they come at your call," Septimus said. "Now, we need to return to the rotunda. I can feel the change in energy from here."

"You never told me about what the rest of the temple is or where it is in this building," Elizabeth said, following him toward the archway.

"There is no time right now, but I will explain as we go. Sometimes it is easier to understand something if you see it rather than me telling you about it when you have nothing to compare it to or to help you envision it."

A flash of cold spiked down Elizabeth's spine and the hairs on her arms rose. The lights over the balustrade dimmed and were overtaken by the swirl of energy and dark light rising from below.

"Come, quickly. There is time yet." Septimus hurried toward the opening over the black star. He disappeared through the arch into the black and blue energy that bruised the air and swallowed the light.

"Oh God," Elizabeth muttered. She took a step forward to follow Septimus and found she couldn't move. A wall of wind pinned her hair back from her face and plastered her clothes against her body. Fighting against the push, she struggled forward, her fingers closing around the edge of the archway. The force threatened to pick her off her feet and hurl her down the stairs behind her. To her horror, voices whispered in the boiling black clouds riding the wind. *No entry...she is weak...she is afraid...she is no match for us...* Malevolent laughter rang in her ears and something inside her shrank from it and the touch of the air on her skin. Septimus' shrill cry cut through Elizabeth's paralysis.

"No!" Elizabeth swept her hands out and down, throwing every bit of determination she could muster into the motion. The wind disappeared with a snap that echoed in her ears. Head held high and with her hands still held before her with the palms outward, Elizabeth ran through the archway.

Septimus stood at the railing, half bent over it, hair streaming in the blast of air rising from below. Elizabeth crossed the Greek Key pattern on the floor, aware of a chill on her skin as she entered the inner circle. She grasped the back of Septimus' coat and pulled him upright and away from the churning mass. A howl of anger rang through the chamber.

"My thanks." Septimus panted while he straightened his clothes. "The Abiff is stronger than I remember."

"The who?" Elizabeth glanced at the boiling ferment rising through the opening.

"The Abiff, come girl, this has been explained to you already. He is the dark, the entity who seeks to destroy all that is good in mankind and turn them to the dark."

"*That's* The Abiff?" Elizabeth stared at the funnel of energy. The eerie otherness of it made her want to turn and run. But run where? There was no place to run, and from the emotion emanating from the pit, no place to hide.

"Not quite yet. This is but a precursor of his arrival, meant to create fear and chaos," Septimus said.

"Well, it's doing a good job," Elizabeth turned her back to the scene to ease the nausea threatening to take her over.

"Yes, it never pays to underestimate the enemy." Septimus took her hands. "But you are made of stronger stuff than that. Come, let's see if we can stop this before it begins."

Reluctantly, Elizabeth followed him toward the spinning mass of chaos which now reached almost to the high rounded dome overhead. Her fingers tightened on the fabric of the man's coat sleeve. Her footsteps faltered the closer they came to the railing, her shoes seeming to stick to the floor, the feeling of lead weights dragging from her limbs. The pressure on her chest choked the breath in her throat.

"I can't," she whispered, loosening her hold on Septimus' sleeve.

"You can. We're almost there." His hand closed over hers and refused to let her slip away. He gazed into her eyes. "You can do this. You are The Elizabeth, he cannot harm you, he can only make you believe he can."

What? The moment of hesitation allowed Septimus to pull her next to him at the railing. She couldn't help looking into the mass of air spinning before her. The weight in her chest lifted and she could move easily again. Startled, she turned to her companion.

"You passed the next test, my dear. Well done." Septimus smiled.

"Great," Elizabeth didn't bother to hide the sarcasm in her voice. "What are we supposed to do about that?" She waved a hand toward the maelstrom before them, now almost touching the pale blue ceiling high above.

"We trust that Athena and Medusa have done their duty in the basement and held back The Abiff's minions there. Our job is to stymie The Abiff's attempt to breach the portal."

"How?" She turned her gaze to the immense power snaking out from the funnel cloud.

"With faith. If we can prevent the spirit from taking his corporeal form, the fight will be won." He gripped her hand and squeezed. "I have faith in you, you are of the Warwick bloodline, the knowledge is strong within you."

"If you say so." Elizabeth wasn't as sure of her strength as her companion appeared to be. "How do we stop him?"

"You will know here," Septimus placed a hand over her heart, "when the time is right, you will know."

A cacophony of roars reverberated through the building, followed by the sound of huge, padded feet galloping through the Staircase Hall. Shrill female voices shouted orders accompanied by the clatter of hooves on marble.

Elizabeth twisted to look through the archway in time to see Medusa race by, mounted on a creature that morphed between buffalo and ox. Athena galloped after her, an arrow notched in her bow. She turned her startled gaze to Septimus.

"Oh dear. It looks like the fight is well and truly joined." He shook his head. "It is more important than ever that we end this now." Gripping her hand, the man brought Elizabeth's attention back to the everchanging maelstrom in the centre of the room.

"What now?" She fought back the urge to run out into the hall and see what was happening there.

"Together, we dig deep into our souls and our hearts, we gather every bit of light, love, and goodness we can muster, and we feed it into the storm. Then we hope that it is enough."

Elizabeth gripped the railing with one hand to prevent herself from being blown away, the other was firmly entwined with Septimus'. Together they leaned into the wild energy. The whip of it against her face took Elizabeth's breath away. She ignored the smothering sensation, holding to Septimus' belief that it couldn't actually hurt her and trusted he told the truth. The sensation eased. Turning her head, she looked into Septimus' eyes, they glowed a brilliant cobalt blue while gold-white light haloed his head. She threw her thoughts at him and felt him catch them, add them to his own. The thoughts melded and became one, light flared around them, static licking and sparking where their hands were joined.

The spinning air seemed to slow, to recede from the heights of the ceiling. Pouring more emotion, more love and light into the synchronicity of their connection, Elizabeth took a deep breath and exhaled. White-gold sparks joined with Septimus' exhalation, forks of lightening striking deep into the blue-black storm. The spinning slowed more, the top of the funnel sinking almost to the height of the balustrade. Elizabeth struggled to hold the connection with Septimus, to continue to conquer the whirling winds. The tip of the funnel shrank below the level of her feet, firmly planted on the floor. Thunder ripped through the night, red streaks of lightning glowed through the windows, followed by a roar of thunder that shook the building. Elizabeth lost her grip on the railing, Septimus' hand ripped out of hers and she found herself airborne, flung across the room to crash into the far wall.

Shaken and disoriented, Elizabeth lay where she fell for a long moment. Shaking her head to clear it, she got to her hands and knees, waiting for the dizziness to dissipate before lurching to her feet.

"Septimus? Septimus, where are you?" Her voice sounded weak even to her ears.

"Here. I'm here. Are you injured?" Septimus limped toward her.

"What happened?" She took his arm to keep him from falling. Elizabeth looked toward the opening within the balustrade expecting to see the churning mass still hanging there. The room was empty. Thunder and lightning still rolled across the sky outside. She wondered if everyone in the city could see and hear it, or if it was confined to their own little war in the legislature grounds. Within the building, but in another wing, the sound of battle cries and curses echoed. It seemed Athena and Medusa were fighting the good fight aided by the snarling and roaring lions.

"Our attempt to thwart the manifestation of The Abiff has failed. He is here, stalking the halls, looking for the key. I was so sure we would stop him." Septimus sounded defeated.

"Well, we didn't. So, what do we do now? What is this key thing he wants so badly?"

Elizabeth's blood was up, and she wanted very badly to do damage to whatever it was that threw her across the room.

"Peace, child. We will not succeed if we do this thing in anger or for revenge." Septimus put a hand on her arm. "I can see your thoughts, feel your anger. You must let them go, for all our sakes."

"That's asking a lot," she muttered.

"Anger and revenge feeds him. We can't afford to give him more power. Light and love and the pursuit of truth and doing what is right, that will defeat him," Septimus insisted.

Elizabeth took a deep breath and let it out slowly. "I guess I can see that, but it doesn't make it any easier."

"Excellent. Now let's go and seek our adversary."

"You're certain that this Abiff character is actually here now. Not just as a spirit but with a physical body? Does that mean he can physically hurt us now?"

"Yes, I am certain he has manifested in corporeal form. Unfortunately, that means he is capable of harming those who are not of the spiritual realm."

Elizabeth whirled back toward him. "Not of the spiritual realm, huh. That's a nice way of saying he can hurt me, but not you or Gramma Lizzy, right?"

"Oh, he can hurt those of us who exist in spiritual form but not as he could hurt you. We must all be very careful. But come, I believe I know where he will look first." Septimus swept from the room without a limp.

Elizabeth followed wishing her bruises would heal as quickly.

"Where are we going?" She hurried to keep up with Septimus' longer strides.

"To where I am certain The Abiff believes the Ark of the Covenant is kept," his tone was casual, as if discussing the whereabouts of the Biblical Ark of the Covenant was a daily conversation piece.

"The Ark of the Covenant? You have got to be kidding me," Elizabeth hissed. "Is this some kind of wild goose chase?"

"I assure you it is quite serious. You do remember I told you this building was created along the lines of a temple, Solomon's Temple to be precise. Hurry, I know a short cut and we might get there before him."

Rolling her eyes in disbelief Elizabeth followed him through a door she hadn't realized was there in all the time she'd spent in the legislature building. The narrow flight of steps was steep and seemed to go straight up. Keeping one hand on the stone wall for support she kept climbing even though her calves burnt with the effort. It was a relief when Septimus pushed a spot on the wall blocking the top of the staircase, which opened a hidden door, and stepped out into an open space. It took a moment for her to realize where she was and then did a double take. The two huge pillars on either side of the double doors facing her flanked a familiar sight—one she'd shown to countless tourists on guided tours of the building. They were standing in front of the Lieutenant Governor's reception room on the east side of the second floor.

"Ah, we are in time. He hasn't come here yet." Septimus nodded.

"What are we doing here?" Elizabeth demanded. "There's no Ark or anything else here."

"Are you sure of that?"

Septimus regarded her, his eyes seeming to ask her a question she didn't understand.

"Pretty sure. Not one that I've ever seen." Elizabeth spun around at the crash that reverberated through the building.

"It would appear that our allies are fighting the good fight," Septimus observed.

"What are they destroying in the process?" She moved toward the open bridge to look down into the depths of the building.

Septimus caught her arm. "Never mind that, we have work to do here." He pulled her toward the dark oak doors. Unhitching the thick rope blocking the double doors from its stanchion, he placed a hand on the door and closed his eyes for a moment.

"It's locked. It's always locked..." Elizabeth said, her voice fading when the righthand door swung open.

The tall man sent her a swift smile over his shoulder before ushering her inside. The door snicked shut behind them. A long desk stood on somewhat spindly legs on the far side of the room before a curtain covered wall that concealed a wide window. On either side of the window were two flags, the Canadian Maple Leaf and the Manitoba provincial flag. Two mismatched armchairs were on either side of the desk pushed back against the wall. A small lectern was situated beside the blue upholstered chair on the righthand side. The walnut woodwork glowed in the light of the ornate chandelier which winked to life when Septimus waved a hand toward it.

"Why are we here?"

"There are things here you need to see and understand. Remember earlier I told you the building was fashioned after a temple?"

She nodded. "There are three parts to a temple building, the Room of Protection, the Sanctuary and the...I don't remember the last one."

"The Holy of Holies. Which is the most important of all. Did you notice the two pillars on either side of the door we entered? Those represent the Masonic pillars of Jochin on the left and Boaz on the right. This room is meant to be a Chamber of Reflection. Notice the mirrors." Septimus pointed to two mirrors facing each other, one on the north wall and one on the south. Notice anything interesting about the mirrors?"

Elizabeth moved closer and inspected the one on the north wall. "They don't match, the frames are different, but aren't they just mirrors?"

"Look into the mirror, what do you see?"

Elizabeth moved so that she was directly in line with the mirror. Reflected back at her was the image of the opposite mirror which was reflecting the image of the original mirror. The complexity of the images captivated her, her eyes seeking more and more reflected images of the mirrors.

"Like looking into infinity, isn't it?" Septimus broke her enchantment with the images.

"Yeah, it's pretty cool. But what does this have to do with the Big Bad we're supposed to be stopping?" She tore her gaze from the mirror.

"This room represents the Holy of Holies in the temple scheme. So, this is where one would expect to find the Ark of the Covenant, yes?" Septimus walked toward the curtained window; his steps silent on the thick blue carpet underfoot.

"Why do we need to find the Ark? I'm still not clear on what we're supposed to be preventing this Abiff guy from doing."

"We don't need the Ark, but The Abiff believes, or so I have surmised from his previous actions, that if he can open the Ark and retrieve what is within he will be given new life."

"I thought the legend was that the Ten Commandments written on gold tablets were concealed in the Ark? How would that give him new life?" Elizabeth was regretting getting mixed up in this crazy escapade more and more with each passing minute. The whole thing was idiotic and beyond belief.

"There are some who believe that the presence of Yahweh, the God of the Israelites, is also in the Ark. That is what The Abiff seeks, and what he must not have."

And we're supposed to stop him? You and me? That's ridiculous, not to mention insane." Elizabeth crossed her arms and paced back toward the mirror but avoided looking at it.

"Us and our allies. Yes."

"What happens if we fail? If the Big Bad opens the Ark and does what...bathes in the presence...eats something that contains the presence...?"

Septimus shook his head. "I don't know what form the presence would take, if any. But if The Abiff gains new life, darkness, corruption, and evil will descend on mankind. Democracy will fail, anarchy will reign, and the world will lose all trace of light, of love, of kindness."

"Oh great, no pressure then." Elizabeth grimaced. "What was that?" She whirled toward the door that was vibrating on its hinges.

"Oh dear. We have taken longer than I meant to here. The Abiff has arrived." Septimus took her hand and pulled her toward the south wall.

"How are we going to fight him? We don't have any weapons, and he sounds pissed."

"This is not where we fight him. The only weapons you will need you already have. For now, we watch."

"Watch—"

Septimus moved closer to the ornately framed mirror. "It has been a long time, but I believe I remember how this is done." He placed his free hand on the mirror, palm pressing on the surface.

"What are you doing? We need to hide somewhere." She looked around wildly. "Behind the curtains?" Elizabeth attempted to yank her hand free of his grip.

"Be still. Quit being foolish." Septimus muttered, still pressing his hand on the mirror and fixing his gaze on the reflections. "Help me," he hissed.

"Help you? How?" She glanced toward the doors that were now bowing inward.

"Your hand. Place your hand beside mine."

"Ok-a-a-y. For all the good it's going to do," she muttered. Lifting the hand not still held captive by Septimus, she pressed her palm to the mirror beside his. His little finger hooked over her thumb.

"Better," he whispered. "Much better."

"I don't see anything bet...." The word better died on her tongue. The glass in the mirror clouded, fogging their images as it did so. Light shimmered across the mist; her fingers sank into the surface as if the glass was melting. She squinted through the thickening mist at Septimus. He met her gaze, his mouth moving, but she couldn't hear the words.

Think of your favourite thing, your best memory, his voice echoed inside her head.

Elizabeth moved her mouth to speak, but found it was impossible. It seemed like her physical body was refusing to obey her. Terror flared in her gut. Was the Big Bad doing this? When she glanced down, it appeared her hand was disappearing into the mirror, up to her wrist. Her body was wrapped in the misty light. She inhaled sharply. *I can see the carpet through my feet. What the hell...* A hard tug of the hand that Septimus still held brought her focus back to him.

Concentrate. I can't do this alone. Trust me. All will be well. The alternative... The amorphous head tipped toward the doors that were even now inching open. *He wins. He cannot win. With me, now.*

Dark lights slid through the narrow crack between the double doors. They soared overhead and the chandelier winked out throwing the room into a twilight gloom. The doors shoved open further and a long fingered hand appeared pushing the doors open. A hooded figure stood for a moment in the opening. The cowl fell back to reveal a cadaverous face. The glinting eyes met Elizabeth's freezing the blood in her veins.

"Ah, at last. The Holy of Holies is mine. You," he pointed at Elizabeth, "you will find it and bring it to me."

The voice demanded her attention, her obedience. She began to fight to release her hand from Septimus. The Ark, yes, she needed to find the Ark. *I don't know where it is*, she screamed soundlessly at the dark figure.

"Don't lie to me, woman. You are The Elizabeth. The Elizabeth knows where the Ark is hidden. You will tell me." The Abiff raised a hand toward her.

Pressure built in her head, blinding her and threatening to split her skull wide open. Elizabeth stopped trying to get free of Septimus and clutched at her head with her free hand.

"Tell me. Show me," the voice commanded.

I don't know! Her voice wailed in her mind. *I don't know.*

"You do. You must tell me."

The pressure in her skull increased. Bright orbs danced across her vision then rapidly faded into black shot through with sickly green lightning.

"Tell me," The Abiff's voice followed her down into the dark.

Elizabeth floated in the inky substance surrounding her. Quite alone, although it seemed that something, or someone, was calling her name. But why go back? It was safe here. No Big Bad, no stupid quest. Yes, yes, much better to just stay right here.

"Elizabeth, you must go back," a woman appeared before her, garbed in light.

"I don't want to," she objected obstinately. "It's safe here."

"Nowhere is safe. Not now. You must go back."

There was something about the figure that was familiar. Elizabeth raised her head and looked at the woman. "Gramma Lizzy? What are you doing here? Did the Big Bad get you too?"

"I have come for you. It is not your time. You must come with me." Gramma Lizzy held out her hand.

"No. I don't want to. I didn't ask to get involved in this stupid war, or whatever it is. I just want to go home."

"You are as stubborn as your great-grandfather, I swear. Darling girl, if you don't come with me now, you will never go home again."

That caught Elizabeth's attention. "What do you mean? That can't be true. All I have to do is wake up from this stupid dream. It'll be morning, the blizzard will be over, and I can go home," she insisted.

"This is not a dream. You cannot just wake up from it. If you don't come with me, you will be caught here forever. Listen to me!" Gramma Lizzy's voice bore into Elizabeth's consciousness. She clutched Elizabeth's shoulder and shoved hard. "I'm sorry I have to do this."

Pain streaked through Elizabeth, her head was spinning, and her brain was on fire. She blinked and peered through the swirling mist of coloured lights.

"Ah, good. You're back. Thank you Lizzy. Come with me now, Elizabeth." Septimus put his hand over hers and pressed hard on the mirror.

Elizabeth realized she was back standing in front of the mirror in the Lieutenant Governor's room. A figure in black robes lay crumpled on the blue carpet a few feet away.

"Is he gone?" she whispered.

"No. We won't get rid of him that easily. But we have time to escape. Quickly!" Septimus looked deep into the mirror while the figure on the floor began to stir and attempted to rise.

"Where are we going? How did you get him to let go of me?"

"Later. I will explain later. Open your mind to me, allow me to guide you. Trust me." His gaze was full of pleading.

Elizabeth was reluctant to trust anyone, but the sight of The Abiff rising to his knees and turning that nightmare of a face toward her made the decision easier. She turned to Septimus and met his eyes. She allowed herself to fall into the deep blue of his eyes.

The mirror under their joined hands flickered and shimmered. Her hand sank through the surface as easily as dipping her fingers into a lake. Septimus stepped forward and brought her alongside. Elizabeth's feet left the carpet, a sense of compression wrapped around her. The memory of The Abiff's hold on her spiked fear in her chest and she struggled against Septimus.

"Be calm. All is well and all will be well," his voice and the worn platitude somehow soothed her fears.

Maybe he's bewitching me, she thought. Septimus rose beside her, both their figures reflected in the shimmering surface of the mirror.

"I'll go first, you will be right behind me. I won't let you go," Septimus promised her.

Elizabeth nodded and fought back the flare of panic when he appeared to slip right into the mirror. The tug on her arm brought her face to face with the fluid surface, taking a breath, Elizabeth dipped her head and plunged after Septimus. He was waiting for her, a proud smile on his face. She had one foot down on the glimmering surface, but her other leg seemed stuck in the mirror. She toppled into Septimus, grabbing at his jacket.

"What's wrong? Why can't I get my leg free?" Panic flooded through her. "Is it lost somehow? Is it just sticking out of the mirror on the other side?"

"It must be The Abiff. We weren't quick enough, and he has a hold of you. Don't panic, I won't let him pull you back through," he assured her.

"How can you be so sure," she asked.

"I am sure because the light will always win. Even though we walk through the dark, the light will win in the end."

"I don't want to walk in the dark, thank you very much," Elizabeth said tartly.

"No, I can see that you don't. In that case, my dear, the onus is on you. Call up all the light and love in your heart and send it streaming through your body and into the part of you that The Abiff has taken possession of. I will assist you, never fear. Our job is not yet done, you and I."

Septimus sounded so sure of himself and convinced of her success that Elizabeth set her scepticism aside and closed her eyes. The pull on her captured leg increased, her body shifted a few inches toward the barrier keeping The Abiff at bay. Clamping down on the spurt of terror and ignoring the throb of pain, she pulled up every memory she could find of what made her happy. Her parents, and grandparents, her dogs and her horses. The sunset on the river, canoeing on Round Lake at the cabin, celebrating the Solstices with friends. Poetry. The light built within her; she glanced down at the golden light emanating from her chest. More light cascaded down the link between her and Septimus. When it seemed like she could hold no more without bursting open, she released it and pushed it down from her heart chakra through her body and into the constriction on her ankle. She allowed it to flow until the pressure in her chest was released and gave the light a final shove picturing it enveloping the darkness on the far side of the barrier.

A scream of rage and agony rent the air. The surface of the barrier flickered, for a moment Elizabeth glimpsed the room they had just fled from where a cloaked figure staggered toward the centre of the room and crumped to the floor amidst his smoking robes. His eyes looked directly into Elizabeth's. *This is not done.* The words thrust their way into her mind before the barrier returned to strength, blocking out the other room.

"Well done, Elizabeth. Well done." Septimus hugged her before stepping back and she could have sworn a blush stained his cheeks. "Forgive me, it I was too forward. I apologize. My relief and joy at your victory make me forget myself for a moment."

"No harm." Elizabeth took in her surroundings. "Where are we anyway?"

"We are in the Mirror of Reflection," Septimus replied as casually as if he said they were in the library.

Chapter Seven

"In the mirror. Of course we are," she said flatly. "And how do you propose to get us out of here?"

"There is nothing to worry about. Being on this plane is actually to our advantage. We can observe The Abiff while he searches the room. It should be somewhat amusing, as he will not find what he is looking for."

"You mean the Ark of the Covenant? He really believes it is in the Lieutenant Governor's Reception Room?"

"He does." Septimus nodded. "It will be interesting to see how long it takes him to find the red herring that was left for him."

"Red herring?"

"Oh yes. There is a perfectly accurate red herring just waiting for him to discover it. In the meantime, let us see if he has recovered enough to begin his search." Septimus touched the liquid surface of the barrier, and it cleared so they were looking from the backside of the mirror into the blue carpeted room.

Elizabeth's eyes unfocussed and she blinked to clear the gauzy veil that clouded the image. She glanced at Septimus when her view of the room was still somewhat obscured.

"Touch the glass," he said, his attention on the blur of black huddled on the floor.

Elizabeth put her index finger on the glass, surprised to find it warm. Immediately the veil dissipated and the details through the mirror sharpened. The shapeless pile of robes stirred, the cowled head rose out of the heap and turned toward the mirror. The material slipped back when the figure clambered to its feet. Dark eyes glared at the mirror with deadly intent. She put a hand to her throat and stepped back, although keeping her other hand in contact with the mirror.

"Can he see us?" she whispered.

"He only sees his own reflection. I'm not sure if he knows what we have done, but I expect he is suspicious," Septimus answered. "This should be interesting."

The cloaked figure straightened to its full height and stalked closer to the mirror, glaring at it from such close range the long nose almost touched the surface, then he whirled and strode to the mirror on the opposite wall. Scowling, The Abiff approached the shining desk and picked up the tall lamp that stood on the righthand side, then he crossed back toward the mirror where Elizabeth and Septimus were hidden.

"What happens if he breaks the mirror? What happens to us?" Elizabeth hissed at her companion.

"Don't worry, dear child. He will not be successful no matter how hard he tries."

Septimus sounded much too calm for Elizabeth's liking. "But what if he does? Are you sure he can't break it? That lamp looks like it's sturdy enough to break a mirror."

"An ordinary mirror, yes of course. But this mirror, and all the mirrors in this building, have been blessed. Nothing with evil intent can harm them. And let me assure you, this spirit has a very evil intent. Now watch."

"Oh my God!" Elizabeth lurched back from the glass. With a mighty crash the lamp rebounded off the other side of the mirror and fell to the carpet with a muffled thump. The glass remained intact without a mark. She moved closer so she could look down and see the remains of the shattered lamp at the feet of The Abiff.

The figure threw its head back and howled with rage. Kicking the remains aside, he tried to claw the mirror from the wall. "I know what you've done, Septimus. Don't think I don't know. I'll make you pay, many times over for thwarting me."

To Elizbeth's immense relief the mirror stayed firmly attached to the wall.

Snarling, The Abiff turned toward the desk and searched through the small drawers before flipping it on its side to explore the underside. The spindly legged chair received the same attention. Tossing it aside, the figure ripped the upholstery of the two chairs that flanked the desk before turning his attention to the heavy blue draperies. Nothing escaped his attention, to her astonishment, The Abiff floated himself up to inspect the valance and the walnut woodwork just below the ceiling. The longer he looked, the more frustrated he seemed to become. Beside her, Septimus chuckled, although Elizabeth couldn't see what was so amusing about the room being destroyed. Robes flying, the figure kicked over the lectern and ripped paintings from the walls. Shoulders heaving, he stood in the centre of the room and then slowly looked upward."

"Ah, maybe he has guessed what is hidden in plain sight above him," Septimus murmured.

"What! The thing he's looking for is in...what...the chandelier? You want him to find it?"

"Oh no, I guess he hasn't figured it out yet," Septimus mused, drawing her attention back to the image through the mirror.

With his robes flowing about him, reminding Elizabeth of great bat wings, the dark figure rose toward the chandelier. He plucked each candle-like fixture from its base, hurling it to the carpet when it proved fruitless. Keeping airborne, he reached out his arms and screeched something in a language she didn't understand. Slowly, the expensive thick blue carpet peeled itself off the floor tipping the results of The Abiff's rampage into one corner of the room. Then it crumpled itself into a septate corner. Dropping back to the floor, The Abiff examined every inch of the flooring. His head jerked up toward the entrance doors and he scrambled to his feet.

The doors burst inward followed by Athena and Medusa, her snakes hissing and coiling on her shoulders. "Be gone," they bellowed. With a twisting snap and one last snarl the cloaked figure vanished.

"Look at this mess," Athena said shaking her head. "What was Septimus thinking to allow this to happen."

"Perhaps the spirit has grown stronger since the last time we did battle. There is much more evil and corruption in the world than before. You can feel it on your skin." Medusa ran a hand over her arm and then stroked the snakes to calm them.

"I wonder where they are, the girl and Septimus," Athena mused.

"Taking care of business, I hope." Medusa sighed. "I suppose we should set this to rights." With a wave of her hands the carpet spread itself smoothly over the floor, pictures soared back to their places, upholstery healed itself, candles returned to the chandelier, the lamp reformed and floated back to the desk and chair that were now upright and unharmed. "I think that should do it. Did I miss anything?"

Athena shook her head. "It looks like it was never abused." She wandered over to the mirror. "Interesting that the spirit was unable to damage the mirrors. I'm sure he would have if he could."

"That is interesting," Medusa joined her.

"Can they see us? Do they know what we did?" Elizabeth leaned away from what she was beginning to think of as a portal.

"No. This is a secret that only I and The Elizabeths know. Those two do not need the mirror's protection at any rate. They are more than a match for whatever comes their way as long as they act together."

"Aid is needed. The Grand Staircase Hall is in danger." The amplified voice of Gramma Lizzy echoed through the building. The two goddesses vanished in a blink followed by the thunder of hooves and ear splitting roars of the lions.

"Should we go and help? Can we get out of the mirror now?" Elizabeth was consumed with the need to do something other than hide behind the safety of a glass wall.

"No, I rather think we should stay right here," Septimus said, his gaze on the empty room.

Elizabeth shifted at his side, wanting more than anything to be racing down to where a battle was raging. She stifled a gasp when her vision was obscured by a black cloud of some smokey material. Using the hand not touching the mirror, she scrubbed her eyes before she realized the obstruction was outside the mirror.

Beside her Septimus chuckled. "We must give him points for realizing there is something about the mirror he doesn't understand and therefore does not trust. Come, we'll just move ourselves to a better vantage point."

"Huh?" Before she could ask what he was talking about, Septimus took her arm and somehow moved them to the mirror on the opposite wall. "

"How did we get here?" She pressed a hand to her stomach which was complaining about the sudden shift in venues.

"It is quite simple. I apologize, I should have warned you. We can move to any mirror in the building. All you have to do is fix firmly in your mind where you wish to go and the mirror you wish to look through. It's simple, really," Septimus explained.

"Simple, sure." Elizabeth was fairly sure it wasn't quite that simple.

"Oh, you're here." Gramma Lizzy materialized beside Elizabeth. "I thought you might have chosen this mirror."

"What the hell?" She jumped sideways, colliding with Septimus whose finger lost contact with the new mirror. The image blurred until he regained contact.

"Easy, girl." Gramma patted her arm. "More than just two can share this space. I came to update you on how the battle is going."

"Oh." It was all Elizabeth could think of to say. Just when she thought this night couldn't get any weirder it threw a new twist at her. *Walking into mirrors, travelling through mirrors? Why can't I wake up. I have to be asleep in my office dreaming all this.*

"You're not dreaming, child. But you are part of a great adventure," Gramma Lizzy said, excitement glinting her eyes behind the old fashioned wire rimmed spectacles perched on her nose.

"Are you reading my mind?" Elizabeth glared at the tiny woman.

"No, no, dear. I would never dream of intruding on you like that. It's just your expression is so transparent it was quite easy to deduce what you are thinking." Lizzy gave her great granddaughter a one-armed hug.

"I'll have to work on that then," Elizabeth said, somewhat mollified. She turned to view the image Septimus conjured in the mirror. A battle raged in the Grand Entrance Hall. Lions and oxen stampeded through the throng of entities who had answered The Abiff's call to battle. Elizabeth turned to Lizzy. "Where did they all come from? What are they?"

"They answered the call to battle, of course. Such as those love to sow chaos and despair in the world. They are the small evils come to life. Hate, anger, madness, jealousy," Lizzy responded.

"Oh, good one!" Septimus cheered as a lion took out five attackers with one swipe, scattering the little demons.

His exclamation brought Elizabeth's attention back to what was transpiring outside their mirror. Some odd sticklike creatures, capering and squealing with their tattered rags flapping around them, were swarming over the wide staircase but were being held back from reaching even the first landing by the swipes of the giant paws of the lions. A small group of children in old-fashioned clothing entered the hall from one of the arches on the side. They carried staves and other small and seemingly makeshift weapons in their hands. The small faces wearing murderous expressions ill-befitting their physical appearance as they joined the fray on the side of The Abiff.

"Where did they come from?" Elizabeth asked. "There's kid ghosts living here?"

"Yes, unfortunately I am not the only ghost in this building," Gramma Lizzy admitted. "These ones frequent the basement area and delight in tormenting the security guards. Especially when a new one is hired and spends his first night shift here."

"But how did they get here? They must have died here, right? I mean to be staying here..." Elizabeth was confused about the logistics. *Are there any logistics concerning ghostly hauntings?* Oblivious to the conversation going on beside him Septimus continued a running commentary on the progress of the battle, stopping only to cheer on a particularly good move by one of the lions and some more oxen who had materialized out of thin air. The stick men were put to route by the two bison's entry into the fray.

"Oh, well done!" Septimus applauded them.

"Well, that's that for now," Gramma Lizzy said.

"The kid ghosts, where did they come from?" Elizabeth persisted.

"I'm not sure. I think there was a terrible accident long before this building was set on this site. I believe those children were orphans and trying to survive on their own. Sadly, they have carried their anger and desperation into the afterlife. From their clothing they appear to be from the late seventeen hundreds. The only name I have heard any of them speak is Stewart, but for the life of me I couldn't tell you which one he is."

"How horrible. Imagine being stuck here and unable to move on," Elizabeth said.

"As for moving on, I'm not sure they wish to. Quite a number of years ago there was a woman who claimed to be a physic who could communicate with the dead. She got permission to spend a night here and try to rid...I mean assist...the children to move on to the next plane," Gramma Lizzy explained.

"And...?"

"Her efforts were quite unsuccessful. By the time morning came the woman was sitting by the entrance doors gibbering away, her hair all coming down around her shoulders and her shawl ripped to shreds. All she would say was the ghosts desired to remain where they were, and it would take a stronger person than she to get them to remove themselves. She fled out the door as soon as she could, and I never saw or heard of her again. The little devils remain in the basement for the most part. They only seem to come up here when something unusual—or that they find entertaining—is going on."

"They are most unpleasant creatures," Septimus agreed. "Thank you for bringing us news," he bowed to Lizzy, "now we must go and find The Abiff. I believe I know which mirror is most likely to reveal him." He offered his arm to Elizabeth. With more than a small amount of trepidation she tucked her hand into the crook of his elbow.

"Always the gentleman." Gramma Lizzy smiled fondly at the pair and then winked out of sight.

"I am never going to get used to that. Not sure that I want to," Elizabeth muttered.

Septimus chuckled and then stepped them into a painting near the Legislature Chambers. The view was a bit obscured by the pigments, but it was possible to see what was happening.

"Where are we?" Elizabeth glanced behind her.

"We can use paintings in a pinch. The glass reflects the light much like the mirror. Not as effective as the painting and canvas interfere. Also, if The Abiff were to realize we were using a painting to spy on him or observe his movements, he could destroy the painting and that would not bode well for us." Septimus peered out of the painting and shook his head. "He does not seem to be here. Pity."

"Bad for us how?" Elizabeth didn't relish the idea of perishing with a destroyed painting.

"The effect would be very disorienting for us. It might take a bit of time to decide exactly where we were evicted to when the painting was destroyed and so it might take some time to find a mirror that will receive us."
"Well, let's just not let that happen, okay?" Elizabeth shuddered. "Can we move to a mirror now, please?"

"Yes, of course. Let's try the upper hallway."

Elizabeth blinked and looked out at the wide hallway near her office. *I wonder if I looked into my office I'd see myself sleeping on my desk. Is there a mirror in my office? I honestly can't remember. I kinda hope there isn't...* A wave of light-headedness stopped her thoughts and flipped her stomach over. She closed her eyes and concentrated on staying upright. To her relief, when she opened her eyes the view from the mirror Septimus took them to was from the far end of the upper hall. Nowhere near her office.

"Well, it would appear he has been here," Septimus said.

"Yeah." Elizabeth took in the upset furniture and dark marks on the hall floor.

"The question would be where is he now?" Septimus frowned. "I don't like this. Not one bit. He should be on this floor looking for the Ark. He believes he can rule if he could only open the Ark and gain the name of God."

"Why does he want the name of God? Wouldn't that mean he would be doing good deeds? Serving mankind? Working with the angels?" Elizabeth tried to puzzle it out in her mind.

"One would think that, yes." Septimus patted her arm. "I believe, and this is only my guess mind you, that The Abiff thinks if he could just capture the name he would be able to either use it to his own ends, or failing that, I believe he plans to hold it ransom or destroy it."

"Is it something that can be destroyed? I mean if it's just a name...how would you destroy a name?"

"I don't know, my dear. As I said, I can only surmise what is in that black heart and mind."

A cold wind whipped down the corridor, frosting the surface of the mirror, it was followed by a cacophony of wailing and caterwauling.

"What the hell is that?" Elizabeth peered through the delicate frost into the hall, but the lights were dimmed to almost nothing.

"Oh dear. That can't be good." Septimus frowned and tapped a finger on his upper lip. "Dear me, dear me."

"What is it? Do you know what's going on?" She gripped his coat lapels and shook the gentleman beside her. Anger surged through her. She was sure there were quite a few important things she wasn't being told about.

"Calm yourself, my dear." Septimus pried her fingers from his coat. "I fear that someone has called the Furies, and they have joined the battle."

"The Furies? You mean like in the myths? What are Roman whatevers doing here?" Panic made her voice rise an octave and she swallowed hard.

"They come when they are called by those who know how to summon them. It seems that The Abiff has been busy in the past hundred years and has made some new friends."

"So, what are we talking about here?" Elizabeth figured she might as well know exactly what she was up against.

"The Furies are goddesses of revenge, or vengeance, if you prefer that term. No matter what they seek, they are formidable foes. They are Roman goddesses, the children of Gaea and Uranus. Typically, they appear as three sisters. Alecto the unceasing, Megaera

85

the grudging and Tisiphone who avenges murder. I think you can see by the last sister why The Abiff relates so strongly to them. Let us hope they are still not speaking to their Greek counterparts, the Erinyes. The three Furies will be more than enough for us to handle."

"How can we defeat them? *Can* we defeat them?" Fear curdled in Elizabeth's stomach.

"Our best bet is Athena. She is the goddess of justice. And more importantly, she holds the key to storehouse on Olympus that holds Zeus' thunderbolts."

"That's comforting...I guess. Do you think Athena knows they've arrived?"

"Oh, most assuredly." Septimus paused and tapped his finger on his chin. "Let us hope...no...no...I don't even want to think it...."

"Think what? If there's worse stuff coming down the pike you better tell me," Elizabeth glared at him.

"Yes, yes. I suppose you are right. I was just hoping that the Furies didn't call on Sekhmet."

"The Egyptian goddess, right? But isn't she associated with war and Ra?"

"Yes, Sekhmet is the goddess of war and destruction, plagues and healing. Her name means The Powerful One. She is the Eye of Ra and the vengeful manifestation of his power."

"Great, let's just hope she stays sunning on the Nile, then. Shouldn't we be getting on with whatever it is we're supposed to be doing? Looking for The Abiff or guarding the Ark or..."

"You are correct. Thank you for keeping me on track. Let's step out of our mirror and make our way down to the hall and see how the others are making out. Once I see how things are progressing I might know better how to thwart The Abiff in his quest."

"How? We just...what...step through the glass?" Elizabeth pressed her hand to the smooth surface in front of her.

"Not exactly. Hold my arm." Septimus crooked his elbow at her, and she slid her hand into his arm. "Just relax and don't fight me or panic. All will be well."

"Yeah, you keep saying that," she muttered and closed her eyes.

Septimus stepped them sideways and twisted to the right. A feeling like the sweep of a waterfall ran over her skin followed by a thump and jar as she found her feet on solid ground once more. She opened her eyes and blinked to clear the bits of mist that clung to her face.

"There, that's better." Septimus released her hand and straightened his frock coat. "Come along. I believe the battle is this way." He strode down the hall toward the atrium where the clash and cries of battle echoed upward.

"Wait up! I'm coming." Elizabeth shook off the lethargy and sensation of displacement and hurried after him.

Chapter Eight

The hallway echoed to her running feet. Elizabeth missed a step and almost took a tumble at the absence of sound from Septimus' boots. The tails of his frock coat stood out with the force of his forward motion, but his boots made no sound, as if they weren't actually hitting the floor.

That's just impossible. She snorted and kept running. *Like anything else about this night is even remotely possible.* She burst out onto the bridge over the rotunda, gasping for breath. Septimus was leaning over and taking stock of the battlefield. To Elizabeth's disgust the man wasn't even breathing hard. *Must be a ghost thing...or spirit thing. I'm not even sure what he is.* She looked down at the circle of the balustrade, it was still stirring with a funnel of darkness shot through with green lightning. She turned to her companion. "What do we do now?"

"We need to join the battle here, I believe. I have no inkling of where The Abiff is right now, and our allies require our assistance. "Come." He strode off the bridge and hurried toward the Grand Staircase.

Inkling? Who even uses words like that now? Elizabeth clung to the incongruity of the word to control the fear raging in her chest. *I so did not sign up for this.* She followed Septimus down the first flight of steps stepping over broken bits of statuary and Lord only knew what else. The force of the malevolence emanating from the funnel of darkness hit her without warning and her steps faltered. Grimly she pushed through the cloud of gloom that threatened to wrap itself around her. Promises of what could be hers mixed with threats of her worst nightmares coming true whirled through her. Elizabeth stumbled to a halt.

"That's correct. I can give you your heart's desire. All you have to do is let me in, open your heart and mind to me. Together we can rule the world as we see fit." The voice became sensuous velvet on her skin. "I can reward those who aid me in this quest. Join with me. When we discover the hiding place of the name of God, all will be ours..." The dark wind teased the ends of her hair, whispered impossible things in her mind.

"Ouch!" Elizabeth yelped. "What are you doing?"

"Saving you from yourself," Septimus growled, keeping a firm hold on the arm he had just pinched. He yanked her toward the top step of the next flight of stairs.

Now she was away from the seductive voice, Elizabeth shuddered and followed Septimus down the stairs where the sounds of battle rang below them. She pulled her arm out of his grasp and scrubbed her hands up and down her arms trying to erase the sensation of the wind on her skin.

"The Pool of the Black Star," Septimus muttered. "As good a place as any to meet the Furies. The altar and the place of sacrifice."

"Sacrifice? Oh no, you promised no one was getting sacrificed." Elizabeth pulled him to a halt.

"This is not exactly the right time or place, but I will try and explain. Sacrifice comes in many different forms; it does not necessarily mean that something or someone loses their life. You have come with me this far, and I have not led you wrong, you must keep trusting in me." Septimus captured her gaze with his own dark one, golden light and flames shone in his irises. "Look at my soul, my lifeforce, if you see aught that disturbs you then by all means abandon the quest."

The flames flared brightly before Elizabeth was enveloped in warmth and love. Serentiy, harmony, and a deep sense of peace swept through her. There was no darkness hiding here, only light and love. She wanted to sink to her knees and stay bathed in the sensations.

"Your decision, your choice?" Septimus' voice broke into her consciousness and the vision faded away.

"Okay, you win. No one dies tonight."

"Excellent. Now I fear, pleasant as this interlude has been, that we must enter the fray."

"Umm, I don't have any weapons. How am I supposed to defend myself?" Elizabeth caught his arm before Septimus could dart down the stairs ahead of her.

The smile he turned on her was brilliant. "Ah, my dear. Your presence will be more than enough. Meet the darkness with light." He swept down the remaining stairs and disappeared into the melee.

"Meet darkness with light...sure, that should stop some monster from devouring me," she muttered. "It's like the freaking Charge of the Light Brigade." Elizabeth kept to the railing for support and to avoid tripping on the debris on the steps. Reaching the bottom of the steps, she stopped to take stock of the situation. Her ears rang with the clash of metal on metal and the shrieks of what she supposed must be the Furies. Three woman-shaped forms swooped and plunged overhead, long tangled hair streaming behind them, their shrieking mouths gleaming with pointed teeth. Leaning down, Elizabeth picked up a long shaft of what she guessed must be part of a broken spear. Sticking close to the wall she sidled further into the round room.

Maybe if she just crept along the wall and avoided drawing attention to herself she could avoid having to jab anyone, or anything, with the pointy end of her pathetic weapon. Didn't Septimus say all she had to do was be here? *Well, I'm here.* The battle raged back and forth across the floor; in a momentary clearing of combatants the Pool of the Black Star came into view. The base of the churning funnel that roared up through the round opening overhead surrounded by the balustrade appeared to originate from the Star. That must be how The Abiff gained entrance into the building, the thought reverberated in her head.

I wonder if I can stop it, cap it like an oil well blowout. I suppose it's worth a try. No one seems to be paying any attention to me. She pushed away from the security of the wall at her back and then hesitated when a huge lion leaped by hot on the heels of three of the child spirits. Taking a firmer grip on the shaft in her hand, she moved forward. *Septimus did promise that no one was going to die. If I'm the catalyst, I wonder if all I have to do is get near to the thing? Or maybe I can just command it to stop.* She shook her head and moved carefully through the throng of fighters, dodging between the combatants. *It's almost like they can't see me...isn't that weird.*

A few feet from the black whirling cloud of who knew what, Elizabeth hesitated. Her skin itched and burned with the bitter wind coming from the Star. When she lifted her foot to move closer the very air impeded her. Struggling against the invisible force she pushed closer. The weapon in her hand vibrated harder the closer she got. Jolts of electricity shot up her arm, and to her startlement the shaft of the broken spear glowed brightly. *Well, that's new. Maybe all I need to do is stick this thing into the tornado thing. Could it be that easy?* Encouraged by the reaction, her previously presumed useless weapon held before her, Elizabeth leaned forward and fought her way to the edge of the Black Star. The cold stung her eyes, forcing them closed. Her hair whipped around her head while the force of the Star plastered her clothes to her body. A deep voice vibrated in her head, speaking words she didn't understand but which chilled her yet further.

Taking the shaft in both hands, Elizabeth lunged forward and plunged the broken end into the maelstrom. The breath rushed out of her body; the shaft torn from her hands. The force threw her away from the Star and slammed her into the wall across the room. She collapsed there, struggling to get some oxygen back into her lungs. An errant thought running through her head finally registered on her consciousness and she shook her head to stop the endless loop. *Nope, not that easy apparently.*

With one hand on the wall for support, Elizabeth got to her feet. She needed to find Septimus, or failing that, Gramma Lizzy. Without their guidance she had no idea what to do next, since her mere presence, or sticking a weapon into the tornado thing, certainly wasn't the answer. Searching the floor, she found a bit of broken statuary, maybe part of an arm, but it had a nicely pointy end and felt good and hefty in her hand. With that in hand, she joined the fray, battering her way toward the Grand Staircase.

"Sorry," she called after bashing a ragged lizard-like creature on the head. "I really need to stop staying I'm sorry," she muttered while whacking another one out of her way. If she could get to the top of the stairs, maybe she could see Septimus, or Gramma Lizzy. Hell, right now even Athena or the spooky snake-haired lady would be welcome. Finally, she reached the first flight of steps and hauled herself up by the banister. She paused on the first landing to survey the melee below. The roar of the lions and the boom of the bison/oxen hooves shook the marble under her feet. From her vantage point it seemed her side was winning. One of the Furies winked out of sight and didn't return, which set her two sisters to wailing even louder. A few of the child spirits were dragging comrades off toward the basement. Overcome with fatigue, Elizabeth forgot about going any higher, the sweep and turn of the battle almost mesmerized her. It was like watching the waves come up the beach and then recede. The vague thought crossed her mind. Her knuckles hurt from gripping the railing to keep her body from swaying. Without meaning to, she slid down and sat on the top step leaning against the railing for support.

"I'm too tired to think and I have no idea what to do anyway," she muttered, her gaze still following the back and forth battle raging below. A shaft of lightning illuminated the entire area followed by a roll of thunder that shook the foundations. Elizabeth surged to her feet while the combatants below ceased beating on each other. As if by common accord, the allies of The Abiff slithered away toward the basement area. Septimus appeared beside Elizabeth as if he had stepped out of thin air. Maybe he did, she thought, no longer surprised by quick appearances and disappearances.

"Come, let's find the others and regroup." Septimus took her hand and led Elizabeth toward the library.

"What happened? Why did you all quit fighting?"

"I'm not entirely sure. It might have been that The Abiff called his minions to discuss future battle plans. But I am only guessing. Let's just be glad it has given us a reprieve for a moment." He paused and glanced about, scanning the groups of fighters following them. "Have you seen Lizzy recently?"

"No. I got separated from both of you. I've been alone."

"That is most distressing. I do hope she joins us in the library." Septimus frowned and quickened his pace.

The library was blessedly quiet and relatively untouched by the battle raging in the building. Elizabeth sank into one of the armchairs, resting her head against the high back. Septimus brought her a cup of tea.

"This will make things better." He placed the bone-china cup and saucer in her hand.

Elizabeth giggled and accepted the offering. "Why is it that all British people think that a cup of tea cures all ills?"

"Perhaps, because it does." Septimus smiled down at her. He took the chair beside her and picked up his own cup of tea which he had set there before bringing Elizabeth's. After a long moment, he turned his head in her direction. "What were you doing at the Black Star? I only realized you were near it when you were sent flying across the room."

"It was stupid really. I remembered you said it was my presence that was important, so I figured maybe all I had to do was get close to the tornado thing and tell it to stop. Oh, and I picked up a broken weapon, I think it was part of a spear. When I got close to the Star the wood acted like it was electrified and it started to shine like crazy. So, when I was standing right near the Star shouting at it to go away and nothing happened, I stuck the spear end into the tornado. That's when it threw me across the room. It's not something I'm likely to try again." She took a sip of her tea, annoyed that her hand shook a bit.

"I see. That was very brave of you, but please don't do anything like that again without first asking advice from myself or Lizzy," Septimus proclaimed.

"Really?" Elizabeth allowed her annoyance and anger to show in her voice. "And when exactly was I supposed to *ask your advice* when neither of you were anywhere around and I was on my own? It was worth the risk because if it worked, this..," she waved an arm around, "would be over."

"I could have told you it wouldn't work. He's too strong." Septimus shook his head.

"You need to tell me everything. You expect me to just leap in and help you with this stupid...I don't know... quest?...haunting? But you won't tell me what you know. Both you and Gramma Lizzy know more than you're letting on. So don't sit there and lecture me about what I should or shouldn't have done." Elizabeth took a huge gulp of tea, glaring at him over the rim.

Septimus cleared his throat and looked down. "Yes, I can appreciate your perspective on this. It's just there are some things that are best learnt or revealed as they occur..." He tapped a finger on his bottom lip. "Yes, yes. I suppose I can tell you this much."

"Great. Spill it." Elizabeth set her tea down and leaned forward.

"Spill it?" Septimus glanced at his half-empty teacup.

"No! No, not the tea. The information." She laughed. "It's just an expression."

"I see. Well, yes, then. The salient points are this: We need to keep The Abiff occupied until almost dawn. I believe his search for the Ark will consume him. We need to keep him away from the rooftop and the Sphinxes. But we, you and I, need to reach the Sphinxes and be ready by sunrise as the day dawns on the beginning of the return of the sun and the Light. Does that help?" Septimus took her hand. "I wish I could explain more, but as it unfolds you will understand. I need you to trust me again, please."

"Let me get this straight. We need to keep the Big Bad occupied and away from the roof. Although why anyone would want to go up on the roof in this weather is beyond me. We distract him with the Ark of the Covenant which he thinks is in the Lieutenant Governor's Reception Room—what you call the Holy of Holies. Then somehow the two of us are supposed to go out on the roof and do something with the stone statues right at sunrise. Correct?"

"That is a pretty concise summary, yes." Septimus released her hand, leaning back in his chair, a somewhat relieved expression crossing his face.

"Sounds like the plot of an action movie. Something some movie hero should be involved in." Elizabeth attempted to reconcile the information with the knowledge that she was supposed to take part in some ridiculous scheme.

"It may be that some movie plots, like myths and legends, have some basis in reality." Septimus regarded her gravely.

Elizabeth started to form a reply but was interrupted by Medusa charging through the door and making a beeline for Septimus.

"It's bad. Oh, it's bad," Medusa cried, the snakes on her head writhing and hissing in response to her anxiety. "Septimus, you must come at once."

"What has happened?" The tall man rose to his feet.

"It's Lizzy, the old Elizabeth. She's gone. We can't reach her," Medusa hissed the words, sounding more like the snakes than a woman.

Elizabeth shot to her feet. "What do you mean you can't *reach* her? Where could she have gone? Isn't she tied to the building and this room in particular?"

Medusa turned her stoney eyes on Elizabeth, whose gaze was drawn to the twisting serpents and their stoney gaze. "They have taken her. It's the only explanation." She leaned closer to Elizabeth, the snakes stretching toward her. "It's your fault—"

"My fault! Wait just a minute. How can it be my fault when I haven't seen Gramma Lizzy in ages? Not since the battle by the

Black Star," Elizabeth snarled back at the animated statue.

"Yes. The Black Star. And what did you do there?" Triumph lit up the flinty face.

"I...ummm..." A hard knot formed in the pit of her stomach. "I tried to stop the tornado thing. I stuck a pointy broken spear into it."

"Yes, you did, didn't you? You dared raise the wrath of The Abiff without sufficient means to completely subdue him. So, he took his revenge and now we must see if we can rescue her." Medusa and her plethora of snakes gave Elizabeth a look that should have turned her to stone but fortunately didn't. "I must go and find Athena and some others." Dismissing Elizabeth, Medusa strode off, feet snapping sharply on the floor.

"Oh my God! See," she rounded on Septimus, "see, if you'd given me more information I would have known that sticking a pointy thing in the tornado wouldn't work. Instead, the only information I had was that *all that was needed was my presence.* What a load of horse crap!" Elizabeth seethed and threw herself back into the chair. "Now, what are we going to do?"

Septimus sighed and steepled his fingers. "We shall go and find Lizzy and rescue her. That is what we must do."

"Fine. Where do you suggest we start?" Elizabeth got to her feet.

"My first inclination is to go to the basement. There are a number of portraits there where he might hide her. It is a starting point." Septimus joined Elizabeth and started for the door. He paused and banged on a table to draw everyone's attention. "The old Elizabeth has been captured. We must find Lizzy and rescue her before our foe does her harm. Everyone, search where your instincts lead you. If you find her you know how to alert the rest of us. On that signal we will all return to this room. Is that clear?" A buzz of assent rippled through the room.

"Good. For Lizzy!" Septimus swept the group with his gaze. "Huzzah!"

The room rang with the rallying cheer from everyone's throat. "For Lizzy!"

Swept along in the mass exodus from the room, Elizabeth kept a hold of Septimus' sleeve in order not to be separated. She followed him down into the lower level where the Manitoba History Wall graced one side of the area and the Keystone Gallery the other. She blinked in the dim light. Huge oil portraits lined the walls and Septimus started at the one closest to where they stood. Although it was relatively quiet where Elizabeth was, the sound of running feet and the murmur of voices filtered down from the upper floors.

"We start here. Look with your eyes and with your inner senses," Septimus instructed her.

"Inner senses?" Elizabeth frowned at him. "Like trusting my gut?"

"That is a rather uncouth way to phrase it, my dear. But, if that makes more sense to you...then yes. Trust your...gut." His expression betrayed his dislike of the term.

"Right. Got it." Elizabeth leaned closer to the painting. "What am I looking for exactly?"

"Lizzy, you daft girl. Lizzy. If The Abiff has taken her into a painting we should be able to find traces of her presence, even if we can't see an image. If he was in a hurry we may be lucky enough to find an image of her and that will make things much simpler."

"Okay, so maybe an image of Gramma Lizzy, but otherwise trust my gut," Elizabeth whispered. "Sure, no problem at all, easy-peasy..."

She leaned as close as she dared to the painting in front of her. A stern looking man looked out over her head. Nose pressed so close she could smell the pigment Elizabeth examined every inch of the portrait she could easily reach. Standing on tiptoe and tipping her head back, allowed her to give the upper reaches of the portrait a cursory scan. Nothing she could discern gave any indication her great grandmother was lurking in the pigments. Or maybe behind the pigments? Inside the image in the portrait? Elizabeth sighed and dropped back onto her heels.

"I can't see anything in this one," she called to Septimus who was starting at the far end of the gallery.

"Keep searching, I feel sure she is here somewhere," his voice echoed a bit.

"Sure," she muttered. "I must be losing my freaking mind. Looking for a deceased–or maybe not so deceased–ancestor in a painting." Still, she moved on to the next painting and laid her hand on the frame to steady herself. The wood was hard and cold under her fingers with no trace of any life force or whatever it was she was supposed to be on the lookout for. Without much hope of finding anything, she raked her gaze over the image. She'd never realized how easy it was to see the brushstrokes in the dried oil pigments and where the artist must have very discretely used a palette knife in the lower corner.

"Nothing." Elizabeth glanced down the gallery, hoping Septimus had been successful in is search but the man had his nose practically buried in the painting he was searching. "Damn." She moved on to the portrait on her right. Something flickered in the corner of her eye when she drew closer. In the dim light of the auxiliary powered lamps, it was hard to tell if what she'd seen was a trick of the light or just her imagination. Elizabeth rested her hand on the side of the frame.

"Ow," she yelped, stepping back and shaking her hand.

"What is it? Did you find something?" Septimus hurried toward her.

"I don't know. When I touched that frame I got a shock from it." She pointed at the offending portrait of a very strict and uptight looking man dressed in the fashions of the early twentieth century.

"Now that is interesting. Let us see if we can repeat that." Septimus frowned at the image.

"Go right ahead." Elizabeth took another step away from the picture. One jolt of electricity was enough for one night.

Shooting her a grin, Septimus leaned forward and with much care placed his hand on the frame. From where Elizabeth stood she noticed a ripple of light flow across the canvas. She caught her breath and squinted in an attempt to bring what she was looking at into sharper focus.

"There." She pointed at a spot in the man's neckcloth which seemed to be where the light was emanating from. "Do you see it?"

Septimus removed his hand and shook it. "Yes, I see what you mean about the sensation. A shock, did you call it?" He came to stand beside her. "That is most promising. Now what is it that you saw? Where was it?"

Elizabeth pointed at the spot where she'd seen the light, but the pigments were dull now and the rippling light was gone. "It was there, just in the knot of the cloth he's got tied around his neck...but it's gone now…" She put a hand on his arm. "Do you think it was Gramma Lizzy?"

"It might well be, or perhaps it only means she was here but has now been moved elsewhere. Would you be so kind as to place your hand on the frame again. I want to see if we can replicate what you saw." Septimus favoured her with a slight bow.

Touching the dratted frame was not high on Elizabeth's list of things she most wanted to do. But, if it would get Gramma Lizzy out of the clutches of the Big Bad and somehow help in bringing this nightmare to a close…. Clenching her jaw, she moved closer and placed her hand on the frame again. Tingles ran up her arm and down her spine, but the sensation wasn't as sharp as the first time, and it didn't push her hand off the wood. "Is it there? Do you see the light?"

"I see what you must have seen, but it isn't very bright, and you said it rippled?"

She looked over her shoulder. Septimus was staring at the man's neck, a frown furrowing his brow, one finger tapping his lower lip. Elizabeth cleared her throat as the prickling in her hand was getting annoying.

"Oh, yes. Sorry. You can remove your hand now."

"What do you think? Is Gramma Lizzy in there?" She nodded toward the portrait in question.

"Not anymore. I do believe she was, but when you first touched the frame somehow it removed her and took her elsewhere. This is most frustrating. While we follow this line of questing The Abiff is free to pursue his goal." Septimus paced away down the gallery.

"Well, we can't just leave Gramma Lizzy in the guy's clutches, can we? What would happen to her if we don't find her and get her loose?" Elizabeth hurried after him.

"I'm not sure what the outcome would be," Septimus admitted. "This is a new trick. One he hasn't played before. I need to think on this…"

"Here you are!" Athena materialized in front of the man. "What the devil are you doing down here?"

"The Abiff has taken Lizzy. I believe it is imperative that we find her and release her, but…what if this is just a blind bluff to distract us…"

"That's what I've come to tell you. Minotaurs have joined the fight in the Grand Staircase."

"Minotaurs? On our side or theirs," Septimus spun around looking toward the upper floor.

"Hard to tell. They're Minotaurs after all. Havoc and destruction, you know how they are. You need to come and assist in planning our next offensive strategy." Athena gripped his arm, and the pair disappeared with a whuff of displaced air.

"Hey," Elizabeth hissed. "For the love of God, this night just keeps going from bad to worse." She glared upward and then came to a decision. "Well, they can just go off and do their war meeting, I'm going to keep looking for Gramma Lizzy. Besides, I don't know what else to do and it's creepy down here. Searching for her will distract me. God, will this night never end? It's like time is standing still."

"Yes, I can do that, young mortal. Make time stand still. Make things appear and disappear," the voice whispered harshly, coming from nowhere and everywhere at once.

"That's nice for you. Why don't you come and face me instead of hiding behind some disembodied voice?" Elizabeth's temper overrode her common sense. Enough was enough. This really wasn't her fight, she'd just been dragged into it, but her conscience demanded that she at least try to rescue her great grandmother. She was family, after all.

A throaty chuckle rippled in her ear, reminding Elizabeth of dry leaves rasping across concrete. "Not yet, young mortal. I am not ready to show myself just yet." The sensation of his presence evaporated along with the faint echo of his laugh.

"Coward!" Tossing her head, Elizabeth glared at the empty space. She might as well keep examining the portrait gallery. Maybe, just maybe, she would get lucky. Although the way her luck was running today... "Nobody is ever going to believe any of this even if I decided to tell someone. They'll think I'm crazy, and perhaps I am. Why can't this just be a bad dream?" Dust rained down from the ceiling as the rumble of many hooves on marble rang in her ears. "Huh, bison/oxen guys or Minotaurs? Take your pick. I should open a betting app and make some money on this craziness," she muttered, no longer disconcerted by the appearance of beings that belonged in ancient myths materializing in the Manitoba Legislature building.

Turning back to the task at hand, Elizabeth continued down the gallery, touching each portrait as she went. The frames remained just that, frames. Cold and inert under her fingers. Sighing, she made her way back to the bottom of the Grand Staircase only to find her way blocked by two ragged children. No, she cautioned herself, not children but spirits of those long ago orphans who perished on the site. Steeling herself for the encounter, she strode forward as if the way was clear. The spirits grinned when she came closer, but her steps didn't falter. Intending to just step right through the spirits, Elizabeth put her foot on the bottom riser. The spirit on the right smiled revealing missing and decayed teeth.

Dread gripped her and cold air misted around her the nearer she got to the two apparitions. Pushing forward, she averted her gaze and took another step. The cold increased, goose flesh rising on her body, but Elizabeth persisted. She moved to step between the figures when a hand closed on her arm. Twisting free, she whirled toward the boy who couldn't have been more than perhaps nine or ten.

"Leave me be. I have no quarrel with you. I am going to go by you," she spoke as firmly as she could manage, pleased her voice didn't tremble.

"We can help you," the second child spirit said, the tremulous voice offered.

Intrigued, in spite of her better judgement, Elizabeth was willing to listen to the spirit. In all the fantasy novels she'd read, didn't assistance often come from unexpected quarters? "How?" She took a closer look at the second spirit while keeping the larger of the two in her peripheral vision.

"We know where she is. We can take you." The small spirit held out a near invisible hand.

"Where who is?" Elizabeth pivoted to keep the other spirit in her sight as it drifted to the side.

"You know who," the first spirit spoke.

"Not playing this game. Tell me who you're talking about or I'm walking up these stairs," Elizabeth fixed the two apparitions with a stern frown.

"Oh, you're no fun." The small spirit stamped a foot. "Your great grandmother, that's who."

Elizabeth was fairly sure now that the smaller one was a girl child, the larger one was certainly a boy, perhaps her brother?

"Ejit! You shouldn't have told!" The larger spirit rounded on the smaller one.

"Sorry, Stewart. I'm that sorry." The smaller figure quailed and grew dimmer and ephemeral. "You gotta forgive me. You gotta."

"We'll talk about that later. You've gone and ruined it. *He* is going to be some mad at us. And it's all your fault!"

"I said as I was sorry, Stewart. Don't be mad at me, please…"

"Who is going to be mad at you?" Elizabeth demanded, interrupting the exchange.

"*Him!* The big black man," the smaller spirit wailed.

"Shut your trap!" Stewart loomed over his companion.

Elizabeth turned her attention to the girl spirit. "What's your name?" She bent down slightly so she was on more of a level with the apparition.

Wiping a hand across her nose, and glancing at Stewart before she spoke, the little spirit straightened her shoulders. "Sarah, don't know my last name, never had one."

"Okay, Sarah. Why are you afraid of the big black man? How can he hurt you when you're already dead?" Maybe reason and common sense would work. If only she could get the spirit things to tell her what they knew.

"He said he could send us back to those men who hurt us," Sarah whispered.

"We ain't never goin' back there," Stewart growled moving closer to Sarah, their disagreement seemingly forgotten.

"I don't think he can. Those men are long gone. Dead lots of years ago," Elizabeth tried to explain.

Sarah shook her head and leaned into the arm Stewart put around her. "Big black man says they're out there waitin' for us."

"We ain't never goin' back to them. The big black man never beats us and we ain't never hungry no more." Stewart nodded his head, glaring at her and daring her to try something.

"Have you ever seen them, the men who hurt you?" She squatted down so she could look directly into their thin faces.

"Don't need to see 'em. I knows what they look like." Stewart squared his stubborn chin.

"You two know you're spirits, yes? That you died?" She bit her lip, how was a person supposed to have a conversation like this?

"Aye, we knows we died alright. And let me tell you it weren't pleasant," Stewart replied.

"Okay, good then...well not good that you're dead, but good that you realize that. So, you're spirits who haven't moved on to wherever it is a soul goes when they die. That means you should be able to see other spirits that haven't moved on. Am I correct?"

Eizabeth was in uncharted waters here and hoping to find a paddle for her canoe that was drifting rapidly downstream.

"Yeah, I guess." Stewart sounded unsure for the first time.

"Then you should be able to see those men who hurt you, or at the very least sense that they're nearby," Elizabeth reasoned.

"Maybe...I don't rightly know." Stewart frowned and glanced down at Sarah.

"Do you think those men are gone?" Sarah turned her grimy face up at Elizabeth.

She nodded. "I do believe they have gone on. If they hadn't you should be able to sense them and if they came near you could most certainly see them." Elizabeth hoped that she was correct, but it seemed to be having an effect on the spirits.

"Then the big black man can't give us back to them," Stewart growled. "Grow ups, they's all alike."

"Do you know where the big black man has taken Lizzy, the spirit that lives in the library?" Elizabeth tried to bring the conversation back to where her interests lay.

"She's nice to us. Makes us cookies sometimes and leaves 'em down by the room where they store all the brooms and stuff," Sarah volunteered.

"That's very nice of her. You wouldn't want anything bad to happen to her would you?" Elizabeth appealed to the spirits.

"Aye, she's nice enough. I guess," Stewart admitted.

"Will you help me find her and release her from the Big Bad?" Elizabeth wasn't sure this was such a great idea, but hells bells, Septimus had deserted her, and facing Minotaurs was way above her pay grade. She waited while the two figures communicated somehow with each other. Finally, they both nodded and looked up at her.

"Aye, we'll help you get Lizzy free. Not because you asked, but I guess we does owe her some'at for her kindness. Me ma always said you should repay kindness with kindness," Stewart said.

"You remember your ma?" Sarah looked up at him with wonder on her face.

"Only a wee bit. Cain't remember her face, but sometimes I can hear her voice," Stewart said.

"Wish I could remember my ma, but I cain't," Sarah's voice wobbled.

"You was alone when we found ya. Weren't no grow ups anywhere around, just you sittin' on a tree stump. That was before them men come along and took us," Stewart recalled.

"So, you'll help me find Gramma Lizzy? You sure you know where she is?" Elizabeth's heart broke for the spirits of the young children, but she needed them to concentrate on the here and now.

"I'm purty sure I knows where he stashed her." Stewart exchanged a look with Sarah.

"Oh no. No. I don't wants to go there. 'Member what happened last time we went there?" Sarah hid her face in her hands.

"Where?" Elizabeth prompted.

"Them shiny mirrors up in the fancy room." Stewart pointed his chin upward.

"Which mirrors?" Frustration edged her tone.

"Them ones that go on and on. Like when you looks into one of 'em it's like yer lookin' into a whole passel of mirrors even though there's oney the two of 'em on the walls facing each other." Stewart shook his head. "Right scary it is. Easy to get lost just lookin' at 'em."

Elizabeth searched her memory of the building trying to remember where she'd seen two mirrors like that. A cold lump formed in the pit of her stomach. Those damn mirrors in the Lieutenant Governor's Reception Room. What did Septimus call it? The Holy of Holies? She glanced down at Sarah, sharing the spirit's horror at the thought of entering the mirrors again.

"Are you talking about the mirrors in the room on the second floor? The room with the big desk in it?" She crossed her fingers. *Please let there be a different room with two mirrors.*

Stewart nodded. "That's the one. I'm almost certain sure that's where the big black man has hidden her. He always seems awful interested in that there place when he shows up."

"Does he show up often?" That comment puzzled Elizabeth. According to Septimus The Abiff was only supposed to appear once every hundred years.

"Not often. Usually, he just comes in the dark when we're restin'. We cain't sleep anymore, but sometimes we like to go into the dark and rest," Stewart said, obviously the spokesman for the two.

"Why does he show up?" Maybe there was a clue of some kind or information that might prove useful later. Elizabeth hoped that was so.

"He tells us to do bad things," Sarah whispered.

"Like what?"

"Scare people mostly. Them guys who hang around here after the place is closed. Sometimes just reg'lar people during the day." Stewart grinned. "We don' mind doin' that, see. It's kinda fun."

"Sometimes he makes us wreck things though. That's not so fun," Sarah offered. "He made us dump a bunch of books on the floor in the library one time. That made Lizzy mad, and she didn't leave us cookies or nuthin' for a long time," Stewart said. "We didn't wanna do that, but he made us and we was scairt."

"If you help me find Gramma Lizzy and get her free, I promise I'll try and find a way to make things better for you. Are there only two of you willing to help me?" The unsettling memory of the feral child spirits armed with weapons from earlier crossed her mind. There might be a whole gang of spirits in The Abiff's thrall.

Another glance that carried an unspoken conversation passed between the two spirits. "There's more of us. Three more. I don' know their names, they never said. I'm the leader though," Stewart spoke with some authority and stuck his bony chest out.

"Will they follow your lead, or will they stay committed to doing what the Big Bad tells them? I saw them fighting on his side earlier." Elizabeth wanted to be clear on that and not get blindsided.

"They should, but you gotta remember, we's all scairt of the big black man. They might not..."

"Good to know. We'll cross that bridge when we come to it," Elizabeth decided. "I'm going to head up to the mirror room, are you coming with me?"

"We'll meet you there," Stewart's voice faded as the pair winked out of sight.

"Be nice to be able to do that. Well, maybe not. Not if I have to be dead to manage it." Elizabeth headed up the wide staircase. The battle still raged in the Pool of the Black Star. The dark wind tornado churning in the centre. And yup, sure enough, two Minotaurs were doing battle with the bison/oxen. Slipping past unnoticed, she scurried up the next flight of steps. Passing the rotunda on the second floor she took the steps to the second floor two at a time. Some inner clock was telling her that time was running out. Only slightly out of breath, she arrived in front of the cordoned off entrance to the Lieutenant Governor's room. Unhooking the velvet rope, she pushed one side of the double doors open, surprised, but somehow not surprised, to find it unlocked.

The figures of the two spirits wavered in the centre of the room. Sarah's face was hidden in Stewarts threadbare jacket. Elizabeth crossed the thick carpet to join them. She glanced at the opposing mirrors and suppressed a shudder. Surely stepping into creepy mirrors should be a once in a lifetime event, not something a person repeated.

"You're sure that's where Gramma Lizzy is?" She bent down so she was eye level with Stewart.

The grey translucent head nodded, Stewart taking great care not to make eye contact with the mirrors. Elizabeth held back a sigh. She straightened up and approached the mirror on the east wall. Halting before it, she touched it with her fingertips. Nothing happened, not even a tingle or twinge. Frowning, Elizabeth placed her palm on the shiny surface below the troubled reflection of her face. Again, nothing. *What the hell did Septimus do the last time? I was so freaked out I wasn't paying any attention and anyway, I had no intention of getting sucked into the mirror-land ever again.*

Frustration roiling in her gut, she whirled away from the polished surface and crossed the room to the other mirror. Her face looked back at her, over and over as the images bounced from mirror reflected image to reflected image, drawing her gaze as the images receded away into what seemed like eternity. Shaking her head, Elizabeth slammed her palm against the glass. "Damn it! What the hell is the trick to this?" She removed her hand and took a step back, glaring into her mirrored eyes. A movement behind her caught her attention. The two child spirits hovered a little way away, their bare feet merging with the plush blue carpet. The smaller one with a thumb in her mouth, the taller one with an arm protectively about her thin shoulders. Elizabeth gave her reflection a last glare before spinning on her heel and crossing the carpet to stand beside the transparent figures.

"Do you know how to get into the mirrors?" Elizabeth knelt in front of them. "Any idea how Septimus does it?"

Sarah shook her head and buried her face deeper into Stewart's coat. The boy spirit's hand absently stroked her head, his face turned up to Elizabeth. "I ain't sure 'xactly how he does it." He hesitated, a fierce look of concentration on his translucent face. "I thinks mayhap the problem is you ain't dead."

"Well, that's a problem, isn't it?" Elizabeth took a step back and considered her options. She wasn't dead and had no intention of becoming dead anytime in the near future. There had to be a way, after all, she had been able to enter the mirror-land with Septimus. She glared at the omnipresent mirror on the opposite wall, then her gaze slid to the huddled figures between her and the far mirror. "Can you get into the mirrors?" she asked Stewart, crossing her fingers behind her back.

"I believe I can, miss."

"Honest?" Elizabeth's suspicions were alerted by the spirit's sudden respectful tones. Still not sure she trusted her supposed allies, she fixed the pair with a stern expression that she hoped would deter them from betraying her.

"Aye, I think I know how they does it," Stewart admitted, casting an apprehensive glance at the nearest mirror.

"Well, how? Spill the beans, boy." Elizabeth held on to her fraying temper with an effort.

"I ain't got no beans. Cain't spill what I ain't got." Stewart edged away from her making the sign against evil with his free hand.

"Oh, for heaven's sake! It's just an expression. Tell me how you think we can get into the mirrors," she demanded.

"I ain't sure. I ain't promisin' anything, ya unnderstan'," Stewart prevaricated. He hesitated for a second, concentration etched on his pale face. "I reckon you cain't beat me, seein' as I'm already dead. And you cain't send me back to them mean men 'cause you said theys has moved on..."

"I wouldn't beat you anyway, silly child. Please just tell me what you know about getting into the mirror-land." Elizabeth changed tactics and attempted to stifle her frustration and reassure the spirits by projecting calmness and kindness in their direction.

"Does we haf to go wif you?" Sarah pulled her head out of the folds of Stewart's coat.

"I would appreciate it if you would come with me, but of course I can't force you to do anything, you know." Elizabeth kept projecting kindness as the ploy seemed to be working.

"I don' wanna," Sarah wailed.

"But I need you both to help me. I can't help make things better for you two if I can't rescue Gramma Lizzy. And Gramma Lizzy needs you as well. Please say you'll be a big girl and help me and Lizzy," Elizabeth wheedled.

"You promise you'll make things better for us iffen we helps you out? Maybe even show us whatever it is we needs to do to move on?" Stewart bargained.

"I said I would," Elizabeth promised. "I never go back on my word."

Stewart stood quite still, considering his options Elizabeth guessed. Finally, he nodded and leant down to whisper in Sarah's ear. She nodded her head of tangled hair and turned to face Elizabeth, standing firm by Sewart's side, her hand clasped in his.

"We'll help ya. Go inta the mirror with ya. But, mind lady, iffen you goes back on your word we'll turn ya over to the big black man our ownselves."

"There's no need to threaten me, Stewart. I said I would do what I can to help you, and I will. Now, how in blazes do we get into the damn mirror?"

Stewart held out his dirty paw and grasped Elizabeth's hand. A chill ran up her arm and down her spine, raising the hairs on her body. Without a word, he marched up to the nearest mirror, Elizabeth in one hand and Sarah in the other. As he approached the mirror, he muttered something under his breath Elizabeth couldn't catch. Then he tucked Sarah's hand into his coat pocket, released her hand, and reached out to the mirror. As his fingers drew near, the glass misted over. Ripples flowed across it as if wind disturbed still water. Stewart placed his hand into the rippled glass, then pushed his arm through the wavering images.

"C'mon, you haf to want to go in. I ain't strong enough to drag you like Septi did." Stewart looked back at Elizabeth; his arm disappeared up to the shoulder in the liquid glass of the mirror.

"Okay." Elizabeth took a deep breath and put her hand into the glowing chaos whirling in front of her. Stewart was enveloped by the radiance, Sarah glimmering beside Elizabeth still. Her stomach flipped and dropped as if she were on a roller coaster, and her head spun so her eyes were dazzled. Suddenly, her feet left the carpet, and her body was compressed on all sides. Sarah's hand gripped hers hard enough to pinch the fingers. A moment later the dizziness was replaced by a sensation of displacement. Elizabeth looked around and found herself peering out of the mirror from the inside.

Stewart and Sarah stood pressed against her side. She smiled down at them in an attempt to reassure them. "Now what do we do? How do we move around and more importantly, how do we discover where Gramma Lizzy is?"

"You're blood of her blood, bone of her bone, ain't you?" Stewart looked at her as if she were an imbecile.

"I suppose so, yes," Elizabeth agreed, not sure what that had to do with anything.

"You're of her bloodline, you should be able to find her through that connection," the spirit said, disgust at her denseness clear in his voice.

"How do I do that?" Elizabeth had no idea what to do, although she did follow the somewhat odd logic.

"How should I know? I ain't got no blood kin. Just, I don' know, close yer eyes and kinda reach out with yer mind and call her." Stewart shrugged. "We gotta move though.

It's dangerous to stand so close to the place you entered for too long. Makes us an easy target iffen anyone is lookin' fer us, like." He tugged Elizabeth and Sarah deeper into the vista of mirror windows that led off into the distance.

"Is there any end to the reflections?" Elizabeth wondered out loud.

"Don' think so. Far as I knows they goes on forever. No one I've heard of has ever gone looking fer the end, or if they did they never come back," Stewart declared. "C'mon. We gotta go away from here."

Elizabeth let him tug her farther into the mirror images. When they were far enough away from the original mirror, he stopped and looked at her expectantly.

"It would be good for you to try now. See if you can find any trace of Lizzy," Stewart prompted her.

"Sure, why not. It's why we're here after all." Feeling more than a little foolish and only a tiny bit optimistic, Elizabeth closed her eyes and tried to send out thoughts toward her great grandmother. She kept a tight hold on the spirits' hands, just in case they tried to make a run for it and leave her stranded in mirrorville forever. A tight band formed around her temples the harder she tried to concentrate. So far, all she could feel was the bit of pain from the constriction, and all she could see was bright spots of light dancing among red spheres on the backs of her eyelids. "This is useless," she cried, opening her eyes to find the two spirits staring at her with expressions of expectation on their grimy faces. The expectation rapidly changed to disappointment.

"Ya gotta keep tryin'" Stewart encouraged her. "You're a grow up, don't ya know how to do this stuff?"

"No, I don't. This is right up my grandmother's alley, not mine." Exasperation hardened her voice.

"Iffen, ya cain't do this, we're wastin' our time and we needs to get out of here," Stewart said. "But ya gotta keep yer promise to help us, yeah?"

"Try harder," Sarah spoke for the first time, her little face even paler that it had been before entering the mirror. "We need Lizzy, she's the oney one whats kind to usen."

"I'll try. Any suggestions on what I should do?" Elizabeth took a deep breath to ease the tension in her chest.

The taller spirit wrinkled his forehead, eyebrows pulled close together over his closed eyes. "Can ya see her? Yer Gramma Lizzy, I mean. I remember somethin' about keepin' a picture of the thing yer searching fer in your mind. Or somethin' like that anyways."

"I can do that, I think." Elizabeth closed her eyes and attempted to bring the image of the ghost librarian to the forefront of her mind. The woman wasn't much older than

Elizabeth herself, although she knew that the woman had been in her nineties when she died. *Hmm, that might be a bonus. Looks like when I get roped into becoming the guardian or whatever, I can pick how I want to appear. I can be young forever. And alone forever, idiot. Concentrate!* She corralled her errant thoughts and managed to bring up a faint picture in her mind of the woman she'd met so briefly earlier in this nightmare of a night. The image flickered in and out of focus before gradually becoming more solid. *Okay, got it. Now what? I just project?* Elizabeth *reached* for the woman with every ounce of her willpower. *Lizzy! Where are you?* Her inner voice was loud in her ears. Finding no response, Elizabeth turned to her left, still keeping a hold of the two child spirits. Nothing. Keeping her resolve strong, she tried another direction. Nothing...no wait... A faint tendril of something teased at the corner of her mind. *Lizzy?* The connection slipped between her mental fingers. Desperate to touch it again, Elizabeth called with everything she had; called until her head hurt. She twisted toward the direction she thought the response had come from. *Lizzy?*

Yes, there was something. So faint it was almost undetectable, but there. Elizabeth opened her eyes. "I found something. It's really faint, but I think it's her. How do we get from here to there?"

"We gots to follow you. You take the lead and we'll foller, make sure nothin' sneaks up on us and follers us," Stewart said. Sarah nodded.

Elizabeth peered into the shimmering mists that swirled around them. "I can't see where to go." She bit her lip. "I think I need to close my eyes to follow the tiny thread I saw. Can you two make sure I don't get hurt or do something stupid like walk into a wall or off a balcony?"

Both spirits nodded at her, looking ever so solemn. "No tricks, missus. We promises," Stewart said.

"I wants to find Lizzy real bad. I really wants some 'a those cookies," Sarah chimed in.

Elizabeth regarded the pair for a long moment, not sure they were trustworthy. However, they were her only hope of finding Gramma Lizzy and, with some luck, actually surviving the night. *Nothing is easy, I suppose.* She closed her eyes and called up the image of the librarian. Holding it firmly in front of her, Elizabeth began to follow the thin silver thread that ran from her mind into the swirling mists. *I'm going to strangle Septimus when I find him.* She pushed the thought away as the thread's image in her mind wavered.

Chapter Nine

Walking with her eyes closed disoriented Elizabeth. She was no longer sure if she was walking on something solid or merely floating along. Fighting the urge to open her eyes, she scrunched her face up and concentrated on the gossamer silver thread leading her deeper into the mirrors. Sarah's hand clutched hers, Stewart kept a firm hold on her arm. The further they travelled, the more the space around them seemed to be shrinking. Elizabeth felt the sides of the frames catching at her sleeve as they passed from mirror to mirror, going deeper into the labyrinth of reflected images.

"I don' think even old Septi has gone this far into the mirrors," Stewart muttered.

The statement did nothing to calm Elizabeth's misgivings. A sense of urgency twisted in her gut, abandoning the shuffling steps she'd been taking, Elizabeth hurried forward. The thread she was following became brighter and wider.

"I think we're getting close," she whispered. Somehow, speaking out loud seemed a dangerous undertaking given the circumstances. "Can you see anything?" She tipped her head toward where she imagined Stewart was in front of her.

"Somethin' maybe," he whispered back, coming to a stop. "I think ya can open yer eyes, missus."

Elizabeth stumbled to a halt and blinked open her eyes. The mist still swirled around them, but it appeared to be thinning. Taking a deep breath, she smiled down at Sarah, whose tiny face was white and pinched with fear. The sight helped Elizabeth conquer her own fear. She was the grownup in the group and therefore the one in charge, or so she hoped. Stewart looked up at her, waiting for her to decide what to do next. The mist was getting thinner, swirling sluggishly now rather than dancing in ribbons around them.

Gritting her teeth, Elizabeth pushed forward and shoved free of the last bit of clinging mist. "Damn it!" Frustration surged through her. There was nothing in front of her except a blank wall. Tension and danger were tangible in the small-enclosed area that was free of the foggy mist. "Something is seriously wrong here," she snarled. Closing her eyes, she reached for the silver thread once more. It was there, right in front of her, leading directly into the solid wall.

"I'm scairt," Sarah whined.

"I know, dear. But be quiet, just let me think for a minute," Elizabeth cautioned the child.

"But I'm scairt. I don' wanna be here," Sarah wailed.

"Be quiet!" Elizabeth kept her eyes closed and searched for the space where the silver thread entered the wall.

"Shut yer pie-hole and quit whingin'", Stewart hissed. "Yelling like that...ye never know what ye might bring down on us."

Ignoring the bickering, Elizabeth studied the image of the wall in her mind. It looked as solid in her inner vision as it did when she opened her eyes. But was it? Considering, she opened her eyes and reached forward. Her fingertips neared the barrier, and it rippled in response to her presence.

"Well now, isn't that interesting?" she mused. Stepping closer, she pressed her palm to the surface. It was warm and yielding under her hand. She hesitated. *Is that good or bad?* They'd come this far, and Lizzy was so close Elizabeth could almost smell the lavender scent of her clothes. Without allowing herself to think about what might or might not be behind the odd barrier, she let go of Sarah's hand and pushed at the black surface with both hands.

"Oh!" Elizabeth leaped back and pushed Sarah behind her. "Keep her safe," she hissed at Stewart. "If something bad happens you two get the hell of out of here."

"We ain't desertin' ye, missus. Yer our oney hope of maybe movin' on, like ye promised," Stewart defied her.

"Your funeral," she growled, "well maybe not seeing as you're already dead, but you get my meaning." Not delaying any longer, she tugged at the narrow split in the wall. "Come on," she grunted the words through gritted teeth and shoved her shoulder into the surface. The wall dissolved in a cloud of dust that sifted down around her feet. "Oh dear. Oh shit," she whispered. "Suppose I should have expected something like this."

Between Elizabeth and the diaphanous form of Lizzy was large woman with a head of writhing snakes. Not one of the Furies that had been doing battle upstairs, oh no. This one was far larger, and she didn't look like she felt like entertaining visitors. "Great, a Gorgon. Just what I need," Elizabeth muttered.

The woman turned on her heel and faced the invading trio. The mouth opened and emitted an ear-piercing shriek of laughter. "Come to do battle with me, have you? Come on, then. Let's see what you have. This guard duty is getting damned boring, I could use the distraction." She reached down and picked up a club with a large spike sticking out of the side of the head. Giving no warning, the Gorgon swung the spike at Elizabeth's head.

"Son of a..." Elizabeth ducked and twisted to the side, avoiding the blow and keeping her feet. Her desperate gaze scanned the area for something to use as a weapon. Other than the club already descending toward her again, there was nothing. "Well hells bell," she hissed, diving out of the way. She stumbled for a second and a heavy hand fastened itself onto her hair. The Gorgon lifted her off her feet and held Elizabeth so she could look directly into her face.

"Hmmm, shall we do this quick and easy, or slowly?" the Gorgon seemed to consider the options. After a moment she nodded, "Yes, yes. Slow I think. So much more amusing."

Elizabeth's scalp was on fire, surely her hair was being ripped out by the roots. In desperation, she kicked out at the woman as hard as she could. A lucky blow struck her captor on the wrist of the hand holding the club which clattered to the floor. The Gorgon flung Elizabeth aside and bent to retrieve the weapon.

Shaking her head to clear her vision, Elizabeth scrambled to her feet. "Stewart! No!" She limped forward as fast as she could manage. Stewart launched himself at the Gorgon, diving on his belly and snatching the club away before the woman could reach it. Sarah huddled as close to the blanket of mist at the rear of the clearing as she could get.

"Mine!" The Gorgon stomped hard enough to send the receding mist into ribbons of darkness.

Stewart struggled backward, dragging the club which was too heavy for him to lift. Elizabeth lunged toward him, but the Gorgon moved faster than she anticipated for a woman of that size and plucked Stewart and the club up in a gnarled hand.

"You think to toy with me?" The rough voice rumbled from deep in the massive chest, the snakes twisting and reaching out toward the boy with their forked tongues.

Elizabeth hesitated just out of reach of the long arms. Now what? A motion behind the Gorgon caught her gaze. Lizzy had gotten to her feet, her figure more solid than it had been when they arrived. *Interesting. Perhaps the Gorgon's attention needs to be on Lizzy to hold her captive. Let's see what we can do about that.* Lizzy was gesturing with her hands but for the life of her Elizabeth couldn't figure out what she was trying to tell her. Sarah crept out of her corner and skirted the Gorgon, making her way to Lizzy's side. The older woman's figure became solid, and she was able to move freely.

"Missus!" Stewart's cry ripped her attention back to the lad still clinging to the club, somehow keeping it out of the Gorgon's reach.

Frustration and impatience with the whole situation came to a head. "Enough!" Elizabeth clapped her hands, the sound echoing like a gun shot. Before the sound had even dissipated a spear of light flared into existence in her right hand. The flame burned cool and comfortable in her grip, and she managed not to drop it in surprise at its appearance. Holding the lance of light before her, Elizabeth advanced on the Gorgon, who seemed to be momentarily stunned by the turn of events.

"That's the bee's knees, my girl," Lizzy cheered, now holding Sarah by her side.

Refusing to be distracted, Elizabeth advanced on the Gorgon. "Put him down," she demanded swinging the lance from side to side.

The snakes appeared mesmerized by the flaring light; their stony eyes fixated on the spear. The Gorgon let Stewart slip through her fingers as she too stared at Elizabeth, the light reflecting in her pupils. Elizabeth used the moments of immobility to her advantage, closing the distance between them. Using the spear to drive the Gorgon to the side and away from Lizzy and Sarah, she hoped that the older woman would take advantage of the opportunity and slip past the combatants.

Stewart picked himself up and dragged the club further away from the snake woman, circling around so he stood nearer to Lizzy and Sarah. The Gorgon shook her massive head, breaking the hold the light had on her and her snakes. With a roar of rage, she sprang at Elizabeth. Caught a bit off guard, she raised the spear and jabbed toward the Gorgon's face, sidestepping the attack as she did so. Stewart ran into the line of sight in her peripheral vision and before she could warn him off, he'd managed to swing the club with all his might, sinking the spike deep into the massive, green and scaly leg just above the ankle. A huge hand reached down and swatted him away. Stewart flew through the air and crumpled into a heap when he hit the ground.

Enraged, Elizabeth forgot to be cautious or afraid. Screaming defiance, she raced straight at the snake woman, intending to drive the spear into her belly, which was about as high as she could reach. Launching herself into the air, she grasped the spear with both hands, putting all her weight behind it. The spear reacted to her rage, burning blue, and then incandescent white, crackling and sparking. She didn't feel the impact of the spear hitting the corpulent body, only the ear splitting shriek and the implosion of power that sent her skidding across the floor to fetch-up by Lizzy's feet.

She scrambled to her feet, groping blindly for the spear of light. Her vision was nothing but white glare interspersed with black spots. Her searching hands found nothing to grasp onto. "Where is it?" She gasped for breath. "Where is *she*?"

Gentle hands stopped her frantic searching. "Easy, child, easy. She's gone. You've won," Lizzy comforted her.

Gradually, Elizabeth's vision returned to normal with Sarah sitting on her lap patting her face. "Where's Stewart? Is he okay?"

"I'm brave, missus," the boy said. He leaned heavily against Lizzy, the bruises already fading from his face. "Cain't really hurt me for long, seein' as I'm dead already. Ye though," he shook his head, "thought ye was a goner. What was ye thinkin' runnin' at it like that?"

"Trying to save you," Elizabeth returned tartly. "No need to say thank you or anything."

"Now, now. Let's just be happy we're all okay and no one was hurt," Lizzy played the peacemaker. "Let's get ourselves out of here and find out what's been happening elsewhere."

"Yes, lets." Elizabeth got to her feet, decanting Sarah from her lap. The darkness was gone and the mists that had so inhibited their initial journey had faded into nothingness. The superimposed mirror images sparkled and shimmered in the pathway before them.

"The journey back will be much simpler," Lizzy assured her. "Follow me, we can just step through the frames now that the Gorgon isn't throwing up her illusions." The slim woman took the lead with the two child spirits after her and Elizabeth bringing up the rear.

"Where are you taking us?" she called to the leader.

"Back to the Lieutenant Governor's mirror, I suppose." She paused. "Where did you last see Septimus?"

"Septimus?" Elizabeth wracked her brain. "I can't remember...maybe in the gallery downstairs in the basement? Yeah, I think that's the last time I saw him..."

"Gracious, that's not good news. I do hope he has managed to keep things from getting too out of hand," Lizzy's voice floated back to her.

"Out of hand?" Elizabeth snorted. "Oh no, let's not let things get out of hand. God help me if they get any more out of hand."

The trip back through the mirrors went quicker, as now she didn't have to keep her eyes closed and feel her way through the stupid mists. The long line of mirror images stretched far behind her and led her onward. She felt like Alice through the looking glass, that old Lewis Carroll book she used to like to read as a kid. Nothing like fantasy becoming reality, she thought wryly.

"Oh, finally," Lizzy said, stepping through the mirror and onto the thick blue carpet of the Lieutenant Governor's room.

Stewart and Sarah tumbled out after her, Elizabeth followed with a bit more elegance, only catching her toe on the bottom of the mirror frame as she exited. Shaking her long hair out of her eyes, she glanced around the room. The carnage that was so apparent earlier seemed to be gone. No broken furniture, everything in its place. She opened her mouth to ask Lizzy how that happened and then closed it. Did it matter? Did she really want to know? Taking a grip on her wandering thoughts, Elizabeth pushed the anomaly to the back of her mind. There were bigger fish to fry than try and figure out who, or what, repaired the damage The Abiff had done.

"Now what?" Elizabeth demanded, joining Lizzy and the child spirits by the door.

"Hush," Lizzy whispered, ear to the door. She straightened after a moment. "I believe it is safe for us to leave this room."

"Where do you think we should go?" Elizabeth asked. She glanced at her watch and frowned. How could it be only five minutes past midnight? The watch was an old one, not one of the digital ones. The second hand refused to move, even when she attempted to move the minute hand manually. "Great, stuck in a time warp. Last time I wish for adventure in my life," she muttered.

"My best guess is we should go to the rotunda. I'm hesitant to go into the Pool of the Black Star unless it is necessary. I have no wish to get any nearer to the origin of the manifestation unless it is imperative that we do so," Lizzy said.

"I'm down with that. The farther we are from the Big Bad, the happier I'll be," Elizabeth agreed.

"Shall we, then?" Lizzy put her hand on the polished brass handle of the double doors. She glanced at her great granddaughter. "I'll go with you, of course. I imagine the children will want to go their own way." She turned to the child spirits.

"Yeah, Miz Lizzy. We'll take our own way, iffen ye don't mind," Stewart agreed. "Be a might easier fer us just pop over there. Kinda quiet like."

"Don't wanna go near the big black man." Sarah hid her face in her companion's shirt.

"Don' worry none, Sarie. Us'll be real quiet. Ain't nobody gonna notice us.' Stewart patted her on the head. His eyes met Elizabeth's, his expression far too old and responsible for his age. "I'll keep 'er safe." The voice lingered while the two small figures winked out of sight.

"Come along then," Lizzy's tone was brusque. "We must find Septimus. Dear, oh dear me. This has never happened before." She pulled the door open and stepped out into the hall, waiting for Elizabeth to follow before shutting the door and replacing the velvet rope across them.

"What has never happened before," Elizabeth asked. "How often have you done this?"

Lizzy's footsteps hesitated before resuming their brisk pace. "To be honest, only the once. But it wasn't anything like this, I must say."

"What do you mean?" Elizabeth was regretting her decision to get involved with this arcane nonsense with each step.

"Well, to begin with. Other than a few times when I left things for the little ones in the basement, I really haven't had much to do with them. They certainly didn't help at all the first time I was called to work with Septimus. And while the Furies showed up last time, they didn't have much effect on the outcome. Not like now, when there's all sort of wild things appearing." Lizzy slowed her pace as they moved past the chamber and approached the open rotunda.

"But you know what you're doing, right? You know what we need to do to get out of this mess, right?" Panic threatened to squeeze Elizabeth's throat, and she had to push the words out.

"I wish I could say I do. The only thing I know for sure is that we need to find Septimus. He is the key to all of this. He needs our help, but he is the key to sending The Abiff back to where he came from. Without him... Without him, I just don't know." Lizzy patted her great granddaughter's arm. "Never fear, girl. We'll figure it out. We're Warwicks after all."

The hollow assurance hung between them as the two women halted and surveyed the round room. The sable tornado still swirled in the centre of the balustrade. If anything, it appeared bigger than Elizabeth recalled, the marble railing appeared to bend outward from the pressure of the tempest it fought to control. There was no sign of the tall man in the frock coat they were looking for.

"Oh!" Elizabeth choked on the exclamation, Stewart and Sarah popped into sight, the smaller one tugging on Elizabeth's skirt.

"Sorry, missus. Didn' mean to scare ye," Stewart said, his eyes on the whirling mass in the centre of the room. The top of the column almost reached to the blue dome overhead.

Lizzy followed his gaze and caught her bottom lip in her teeth. "Oh, my stars. That is not good. Not good at all."

"What isn't, or should I say, what else isn't?" Elizabeth looked up as well.

"The whirlwind. I think it will go very badly for us should it reach the top of the dome. The figure of Eternal Youth is right above that. It must be protected. Oh, we must find Septimus." Lizzy twisted her hands in her pockets.

"Why is it so important we protect a statue?" Elizabeth demanded, then changed her mind. "You know what? It doesn't matter. Let's just get on with it and find Septimus." She turned to the two spirits. "Have you seen him? Have any idea where he might have gone?"

Stewart started to shake his head when Sarah tugged at his sleeve. He bent down so she could whisper in his ear.

"Yer sure?" He straightened up, a confused expression on his face.

She nodded. "Sure, as sure."

"What's she sure of?" Elizabeth knelt by the small figure.

Stewart shrugged his thin shoulders. "She says he went outside—"

"Outside! Outside where? He left the building?" Lizzy's eyes widened in disbelief and fear.

"No, Miz Lizzy. He ain't left the buildin'. But Sarah says he's outside." He bent down again Sarah tugged on his arm and whispered in his ear again. "He's on the...roof?"

Sarah nodded so hard her tangled hair bounced on her shoulders.

"What in God's name is he doing on the roof?" Elizabeth muttered. "And in this storm?"

Lizzy knelt by Sarah and took her tiny hands in hers. "Where is he on the roof, Sarah? Can you tell me? It's so very important. You're sure he's on the roof of this building right now?"

"Yes, 'em. I'se sure," Sarah whispered.

"Can you tell me where exactly he is?" Lizzy prompted her.

The tiny gossamer features crinkled in concentration. She closed her eyes for a moment, then nodding her head, she opened them. "He's up there." She pointed toward the ceiling. By a big stone box. It's gots two men around it. One of them chief men and another guy with wings on his head."

"You're sure Septimus is there too. Can you see him?" Lizzy dug for more information.

"He's there alright. He's fightin' with the big black man." Sarah clung to the older woman. "I don' wants 'im to gets hurt, so I don'."

"We gotta go help," Stewart declared and headed off toward the east side of the speaker's gallery, taking Sarah with him.

"Where are you going?" Elizabeth followed them. "How do you know where he is?"

"Oh my God!" Lizzy exclaimed. "He's by the War Chest. I have no idea how to get up there to help."

"Hold on. What in the hell is the War Chest?"

"C'mon, there ain't much time," Stewart cried. He stood beside what appeared to be a solid wall.

"I'm not going anywhere until I get some answers. What is this war chest and why is it on the roof of the building?" Elizabeth stood her ground. Enough was enough. Following on blind faith wasn't something she was comfortable with.

"The War Chest is on the east pediment, right under the statue of Eternal Youth. I know it has the same dimensions as the Ark of the Covenant because Septimus told me one time. The two men on either side take the place of the cherubim who guarded the actual Ark in the Bible. I suppose the architect thought that a native chief guardian was more appropriate for Winnipeg but why on earth he chose to put what looks to me like a Roman soldier on the other side is beyond me. Septimus would never explain that to me. The War Chest is above Lieutenant Governor's room, which makes sense I suppose since Septimus calls that room the Holy of Holies."

"So, you're saying we need to somehow get up on the roof in this storm and help Septimus fight the Big Bad? Why are they fighting in the first place? Is there something in the stone chest?" Every ounce of sense in Elizabeth's body was telling her the idea of going up on the roof in the middle of a blizzard was insanity.

"I think that's exactly what we need to do. I don't believe there is anything hidden in the chest, but of course, I could be mistaken. I also have no idea why they would be fighting over it, but I can only surmise that it must be very important to both parties. And since we are allied with Septimus, whatever it is must also be important to us." Lizzy shook her head and raised her hands in surrender. "I'm afraid I can't enlighten you any more than that."

"Oh hell," Elizabeth muttered. "I don't suppose I can get out of this time warp until we settle this." She nodded at Lizzy. "Okay, I'm in."

"Are ye gonna stand there jawin' all night? We gots to go!" Stewart was practically dancing on the spot in desperation.

"We're coming," Elizabeth assured him. She swept the area for a door that might lead to a staircase that would take them to the roof.

"Over here," Stewart shouted.

A loud blast followed by a sharp gust of air swept up from the Pool of the Black Star below them. The roiling funnel in the centre of the rotunda faltered for a brief second and then regained its strength. If anything, instead of weakening, the speed of the winds accelerated.

"Hurry up! Over here." Stewart shoved at an odd symbol on a stone pillar at the edge of the room. The stone moved under his hand, revealing a narrow entrance. "In here!"

"My stars! I never knew such a thing existed." Lizzy hurried toward the two spirits. "You're sure this will take us up to the War Chest?"

Stewart nodded. "C'mon. No time fer dilly-dallying. Septi needs our help." He drew Sarah with him into the dim interior of the staircase.

Elizabeth exchanged a worried look with Lizzy, then shrugged and stepped onto the first narrow riser. There was no handrail, the stairs led upward at a sharp angle and Elizabeth wished for the flashlight on her cell phone which, she supposed, was still sitting on her desk. *Bother and damn.*

"How do you know about this stairway?" Lizzy called up to Stewart.

"I seen Septi use it a time or two. And some workie gents uses it sometimes. Get's purty borin' in the cellars, so I goes 'splorin' when it suits me," his voice floated back to the two women.

Elizabeth snorted and kept climbing. It seemed like, ghost or no ghost, boys would be boys.

"Well, I never," Lizzy muttered.

The stairs seemed to go up for far too long as far as Elizabeth was concerned. Encased in the thick stone walls of the building the howl of the blizzard was non-existent. Perhaps it had blown itself out? She could only hope that it was so. A shudder ran through her when she collided with the two spirits who halted in front of her. Elizabeth drew back a step and moved aside so that Lizzy could join them on the tiny landing.

"How do we get out?" Elizabeth asked.

"Easy, we jes gots to shove on this here thingy." Stewart gestured at a lever on the flat surface before them.

"Then what? Where do we come out?" Lizzy wiggled her way to the front of the group.

Stewart shrugged. "Don' know. Never went no further than this."

"All right, then. I'll go first." Lizzy glanced at Elizabeth. "No point having you step out into nothing if there's no place to perch once we open the door."

"Good point. I'm the only one of us who can actually die." The comment struck

Elizabeth as somewhat amusing given the circumstances and she fought back a hysterical giggle. "Be my guest." She gestured toward the lever.

Lizzy placed her hand on the wall and a portion of it slid back into itself without a sound. A smattering of snow blew through the opening, but to Elizabeth's surprise, only a tiny movement of air accompanied it. She peered over Lizzy's shoulder.

The blizzard was still howling over downtown Winnipeg. Her Winnipeg, she was relieved to discover. Not the Winnipeg of the 1920s. Before them, there was an area of calm air surrounding the stone chest perched right on the edge of the pediment. Above them wind, whirled around the icy Eternal Youth statue. The gold colouring was almost obscured by the coating of snow that adorned it.

"What should we do?" Elizabeth whispered to Lizzy.

She hovered in the relative safety of the landing. Two figures struggled by the stone chest, somehow not toppling off the narrow ledge on each side of the guardian figures. Her first clear view of The Abiff sent shivers down Elizabeth's spine that had nothing to do with the air temperature. The sheer alienness of him robbed her of movement, the hairs on her arms quivering erect. Her gaze slid to Septimus, his coat tails swishing behind him as he sparred with The Abiff. In his hands was a glowing sphere of light which waxed and waned as the two circled each other. For the life of her, Elizabeth couldn't understand how the pair were staying stable and not plummeting to earth.

Lizzy stepped out onto the pediment, fighting the winds until she gained the safe haven of calm that surrounded the combatants. Raising her hands, she called up a sword of blue-white light and moved to Septimus' side. The black figure hesitated for a moment but then renewed his attack. To Elizabeth's eyes, the Big Bad seemed to be trying to reach the guardian figures on either side of the chest. She hovered in the doorway, pushing the two child spirits behind her. The storm battered at the edges of the bubble of protection but had no effect on the battle raging inside. Fear sent her heart beating erratically in her chest and she forced herself to breathe through the panic.

How am I supposed to help? It feels like I need to be here, but I have no idea what it is I'm supposed to do. Elizabeth hesitated to call out to either Septimus or Lizzy in case she distracted them at a critical moment. Lightening split the clouds, liming the golden statue in brilliant light. Septimus used the distraction to force the black figure off the pediment, but instead of falling, The Abiff hung in mid-air and then calmly settled back onto the building. A black staff, sizzling with some sort of electric charge, sparked in his grasp.

"Oh, that can't be good," Elizabeth whispered and turned to the spirits behind her. "Maybe you should go back down to the basement. It's probably safer there."

Stewart shook his head. "Nah, we ain't goin' anywhere. I'm aimin' to make sure ye keep yer promise to help us move on. Ain't lettin' ye out of me sight until ye does that."

"Oh, for heaven's sake. I promised I'd do my best to help you." She shrugged in frustration. "Go or stay, up to you." Elizabeth turned her attention back to the battle.

The Abiff made a swooping move to bring the black staff close to the headdress of the nearest guardian. To Elizabeth's horror, the figure quivered as if the stone was trying to move. With a cry, Lizzy swung her sword and cut through the connection between the black staff and the statue. On the opposite side of the chest, Septimus now repeated the action as the black staff was aimed at the Roman soldier. Frustrated for the moment, The Abiff drew back and seemed to be waiting for his two foes to make a move.

"What can I do to help?" Elizabeth shouted at her allies. Somehow standing huddled safely in the doorway seemed cowardly. Although keeping her skin in one piece was also a priority. Something she didn't think the other combatants had to worry about. *I mean, they're already dead. Right?*

Septimus blocked a surprise strike from The Abiff while Lizzy whirled to guard the plumed soldier. Elizabeth stepped into the combat zone, amazed at how warm the temperature in the secure bubble was. Sweat immediately beaded on her forehead.

"You need to get close enough to touch the guardians. One at a time," Septimus grunted the words between blocking blows of the black staff.

"It must be you, Elizabeth. It needs the touch of a mortal," Lizzy called as she moved to assist Septimus.

Elizabeth slipped behind Lizzy and attempted to sidle closer to the stone chest. A blood-curdling roar swept over her, the sound actually having a physical presence. How is that possible, she wondered while her steps faltered. Ducking under Septimus' staff of white light, she edged closer to the native on the side of the chest closest to her. A blast of sound from The Abiff shoved her back a step. She lowered her head and pushed forward.

"Almost there." Lizzy gasped for air pausing to catch her breath. "Almost there, child. You can do this. You must."

"Sure, easy for you to say," Elizabeth muttered. The air misted around her, somehow the black spirit was lowering the air temperature. She blinked and shuffled her feet forward. There was very little room on the pediment and there was no way she was going to get down on the thin ledge where the others fought. Fine for them, if they slipped off, they just hung in the air until they could regain their footing. If Elizabeth slipped...well, it was a long way to the ground with no guarantee a friendly snowbank would catch her.

Ducking again, she threw herself flat on the area behind the stone chest. If she could just creep close enough, Elizabeth was fairly sure it was possible to reach over the top and touch the headdress of the native. Maybe. Inching forward, she kept her gaze firmly on her goal. The urge to look up and gauge where the others were was almost irresistible. She flinched at every boom and sizzle of the weapons connecting, sure that the next blow would be on her head. Holding her breath, her fingers found the top of the pediment.

"Look out!"

Septimus' shout came just in time for her to avoid a strike by the black staff that hit the stonework instead with a blaze of sparks. Swallowing her fear, Elizabeth inched back to her position and shoved her arm over the side as far as she could manage. Her fingers scrabbled on stone, but nothing happened other than she broke a nail. *Damn it*. She risked a quick look. Her fingers rested on the stone drum that stood on top of the chest. She was too far to the right. Withdrawing her hand, Elizabeth wriggled her way toward the stern-faced statue crowned with the huge headdress. She kept her head down until she estimated she was close enough. She peered over and extended her arm, fingers finding the carven feathers.

A jolt of energy flung her hand away, light flared, blinding her. A cry of rage echoed and pushed against the protective barrier around them. Elizabeth waited for her vision to clear before attempting to look up. The guardian in the headdress got to his feet, stone flexing and moving as easily as if it were flesh and blood. He picked up something from the top of the chest which burst into flame and joined the battle. The three allies circled The Abiff who appeared only mildly concerned, was still attempting to reach the Roman soldier guardian. His insistence on gaining access to the other guardian spurred her into action.

Elizabeth checked her hand that was still tingling from waking the first guardian, wiggling her fingers. To her surprise, there was no blackened skin or blisters from the flare of light. Just a lingering fizz of power. Emboldened by her success, she edged toward the soldier, while keeping an eye on the four combatants. With the three allies to keep The Abiff occupied, it wasn't as chancy to try and reach the plumed helmet.

"Close, so close," she hissed between her teeth. A peal of thunder ripped through the storm outside the bubble fed by The Abiff's anger. It seemed to give the black staff power as it grew thicker and gave off more energy in response to the boom. Lizzy stumbled and almost fell, Septimus moved to guard her back, leaving The Abiff with only the one guardian to deal with. Elizabeth made a desperate lunge toward the far side of the chest. Her attention was riveted on the plumed helmet. She reached, and overbalanced, tipping off the pediment. Her hands scrabbled for purchase on the curved plume as she passed it, then slid off the shoulder. The jolt of energy threw her away from the statue, the light blinding her again.

"Oh, God. Oh, God. I'm gonna fall." The words were torn from her lips. It felt like slow motion as she hit the narrow ledge by the statue's feet and bounced off. The blizzard enveloped her, and Elizabeth squeezed her eyes shut in expectation of the stomach churning drop that was surely coming her way. The wind and snow buffeted her and whirled her about. *Is the wind strong enough to keep me from falling? What the hell?*

The collar of her blouse cut into her neck while she was roughly jerked back into the semi-calm of the bubble. The sharp pain in her butt when she landed on a hard surface popped her eyes open. She looked up into the grinning face of the Roman soldier. He nodded at her, produced a long sword that shone with an unearthly bronze light and leaped into the fray. Elizabeth pulled the collar of her blouse away from her bruised neck and got to her feet. She was only a few steps from the opening to the narrow staircase. Her first instinct was to bolt down the passageway, find her way to the legislature's main doors, and beat on them until they opened. She moved as far as the door, which, thankfully, still stood open. The shadowy figures of Stewart and Sarah hovered just inside. Their presence stopped her panicked flight.

"Did ye see that? That stone guy saved ye," Stewart declared. "I ain't never seen nothin' like that afore."

"Ye was so brave," Sarah said, looking up at Elizabeth with an adoring expression lighting her face. "Wish I was that brave."

"You are brave," Elizabeth insisted. "Both of you. You could have run for it, but you stayed here. I'm very proud of both of you."

She turned at the strident clash of weapons that increased in ferocity. The four allies had The Abiff surrounded, but somehow he slipped past them and plunged his hands deep into the stone chest. All activity ceased, even the storm seemed to pause. Septimus stepped back with a satisfied expression on his face. He straightened his frock coat and settled his top hat back on his head. Fear speared through Elizabeth. Was Septimus changing sides? Was he really on the side of the dark? What a fool she was not to have even thought something like that might be true.

The Abiff threw back his head and howled with rage. He pulled his arms out of the stone chest as easily as if it was liquid. He whipped around and threw the black staff at Septimus.

"You! You call me wicked. You lied to me. You led me to believe this," he spit on the stone chest, "was the Ark of the Covenant that I seek. That I would find what I sought here." The eyes glittered with black and red lights above the long beard, lips drawn back in a snarl.

Septimus avoided the main thrust, the staff only passing through the tail of his coat as he moved away. "You heard what you wished to hear. I promised you nothing. What you seek is not yours to find. You gave up the right to reclaim that which you seek when you embraced the dark."

"You know nothing of what I have suffered. Of what I am owed," the bitter words ripped from his mouth. Another black staff materialized in his left hand. With another curse, he slammed the butt of the staff on the stone. When the light and concussion of sound faded, they were alone on the pediment.

Septimus turned to the guardians. "I thank you for your assistance. It was most appreciated and certainly helped turn the tide."

"Yes, without you we would have been hard pressed to turn him aside," Lizzy said, coming to stand beside Septimus.

"It is we who should be thanking you. That was the most fun we've had in ages," the Roman soldier said.

"Yes, it gets monotonous just sitting up here guarding the stone chest that really needs no guarding," the native chief said, straightening a few feathers on his headdress.

"What do you mean it doesn't need guarding?" Elizabeth demanded. "What was all the fighting about if it didn't matter if he got into it?

"Now, I didn't say it didn't matter. On this night it does need to be watched and protected. But for most of the time it is just what it seems...a stone chest," Septimus said.

"And?" Elizabeth had no intention of letting him off that easily. "Spill. Why the big battle then?"

"The stone chest, the War Chest as it is known, on this night becomes a red herring. A diversion to keep The Abiff from searching where this is something he might find. Something we don't wish him to touch. He has gone now to gnash his teeth and lick his wounds. We'll take the opportunity to regroup and then we will prepare for the final battle. This night is a long way from over," Septimus replied.

The Roman soldier flexed his arms and sighed. "I fear it is time for me to return to my duty." He moved to his vacated place by the chest and squatted down, resting one elbow on the edge.

"I also," the chief agreed, moving to his former position.

"Once again, my thanks to you both," Septimus said with a slight bow.

Lizzy ran a hand over both men's shoulders, the supple flesh returning to stone, the light fading from the eyes.

Elizabeth hovered by the doorway with the child spirits. Lizzy and Septimus joined her, and they made their way down the narrow stairs. When they reached the bottom and stood once more in the hall by the speaker's chambers, Septimus laid a hand on the wall to close the hidden doorway.

"I've worked in this building for over three years, and I never knew that existed," Elizabeth remarked. "Does anyone besides you spirits know it's there?"

"Only you, dear child," Lizzy said. "Only you. And when the time comes, it will be revealed to your successor, just as it has been revealed to you."

"Huh." Elizabeth mulled that over in her mind.

The sounds of fighting down in the Pool of the Black Star seemed to have dissipated. No clash of weapons rose from the floor below, although the whirlwind still occupied the centre of the balustrade.

"Come. Let's retire to the library. I believe Lizzy can brew us up a cuppa and maybe find some biscuits," Septimus said.

"A capital idea," Lizzy agreed. "I'm sure the littles are wanting something sweet by now." She smiled down at the two little spirits.

"Yes, please," Sarah said and slipped her hand into Lizzy's.

Shaking her head, Elizabeth followed the strange entourage down to the library. Who knew child ghosts like cookies?

Chapter Ten

Comfortably seated in an overstuffed armchair, Elizabeth sipped tea out of the delicate china cup Lizzy produced from some unknown source. Stewart and Sarah, curled together in the seat opposite her, were scarfing down cookies. Elizabeth pondered the paradox of the children, who were for all intents and purposes dead, eating cookies. Cookies that another ghost baked for them. Presumably in a ghost oven? Shaking her head, she dismissed the thought from her mind. Bigger fish to fry, she reminded herself.

Setting the fragile cup in the saucer and placing both on the table at her side, Elizabeth leaned forward. "Where do we go from here? You indicated there was more nastiness coming earlier. You mentioned some kind of fish? What did you mean?"

"Ah yes. The red herring. It was something we needed to do, distract The Abiff and keep him from realizing too soon that the War Chest was a dead end." He glanced at the clock on the library wall—the only one Elizabeth had seen that actually worked since this whole craziness started.

"We have time now for me to explain further. Do you agree, Lizzy?"

"I do think it is time that we explained everything to my great granddaughter, the poor girl." Lizzy perched on the edge of her chair, setting her cup of tea on the long table in front of her. She nodded at Septimus to begin.

"Much of this you know, so I won't start at the beginning but go on from where we are at the moment. Does that suit?" He paused and waited for Elizabeth to nod. "Excellent. An important thing to point out is that The Abiff does not seem to remember from one manifestation to the next what has occurred in the past. For example, when Lizzy was in your place, one hundred years ago this night, we fought at the War Chest with the same results. Eventually, The Abiff got his hands on the chest and discovered it contained nothing that he was interested in—"

"Wait," Elizabeth interrupted him, "I thought Hiram Abiff, the original guy who was murdered...didn't he know the name of God? Wasn't that what those three 'J' guys murdered him trying to find out?"

"Yes, that's so. Hiram Abiff did indeed know the true name of God," Septimus said.

"Isn't that what this spirit Abiff is looking for? Thinking the War Chest, or the Ark of whatever, holds that secret? Why doesn't he remember it himself? From what I gathered from you, this spirit is the remains of the original Hiram. I guess I just don't understand...

"As I said, this manifestation is, in part, Hiram Abiff. But somewhere along the way, he lost all that was good and right and the only thing remaining is the anger and rage of his murder. I believe when he discarded, or lost if you will, decency and righteousness, that he also lost the knowledge he held most dear. The knowledge of the true name of God."

"And so now he wants that knowledge back," Elizabeth guessed.

"More than anything in the world," Lizzy said.

"But if he remembered what it was, wouldn't that be a good thing? Wouldn't he turn back into the faithful servant of God that he was?" Elizabeth turned to Septimus for his thoughts.

"Would that it were so. I fear the dark powers that rule The Abiff want only to turn it to their own uses. Hate and Love are very similar in their intensity. Love can be turned to Hate, and vice versa. And for some reason, hate and the darkness it holds always seems to hold sway over those who have come to see the dark as power which they can use for their own selfish reasons." Septimus shook his head. "But we digress. There are things you need to know before the final fight is joined."

"Oh, one more thing. Why doesn't my watch work? The clock in here seems to be keeping time, but anything outside of this room seems to have stopped at three minutes after midnight," Elizabeth said.

"This room is a sanctuary. It is protected by my presence as the guardian. I am The Elizabeth, as you will be in your turn," Lizzy reminded her. "Outside of this space, the time is held in abeyance until the final act is complete, for good or ill."

"That sounds ominous." Elizabeth sat back in her chair and reached for her tea. She sighed. "What is that I need to know, then?"

"As you know, this occurs only once every hundred years. This is only the second occurrence since the building was completed, but the struggle between good and evil, the light and the dark, will go on long after the stones are turned to dust. For now, it falls on our shoulders and those of our ancestors to protect that which is entrusted to us."

"Sure, okay. But what exactly are we, am I, supposed to do?" Frustration laced Elizabeth's tone. "Enough beating around the bush, it's not like I'm gonna bolt on you at this point."

"Very well. We must be up on the roof when the sun rises in the east at the close of the longest night—"

"Oh no." Elizabeth got her feet and paced back and forth. "No way am I going out on that roof again. Uh uh. No way."

"You must. You must." Lizzy grabbed her hands, halting her frantic movements.

"You will be quite safe, my dear," Septimus assured her.

"You can't guarantee that though, can you? What if the Big Bad shows up? I almost fell off the roof last time. If it wasn't for the stone centurion guy I would have face-planted in a snowbank." Elizabeth glared at Septimus.

The tall gentleman exchanged a long look with Lizzy. "That was most unfortunate, I agree..."

"Unfortunate! Really, that's all you can say? Unfortunate?" Elizabeth snorted and pulled her hands away from Lizzy.

"Be calm, dear. It's my duty to ensure the safety of those who touch the Truth. At this juncture in the events, I will have the help of the elements. Here the true meaning of the Golden Boy, Eternal Youth is revealed. There are four stone works, one each on the four corners of the central square tower which supports the dome. Some refer to them as Science, Industry, Art and Agriculture. To those of us with the esoteric knowledge, we recognize them as Air which is represented by Science, Fire which is represented by Industry, Water which is represented by Art, and Earth which is represented by Agriculture. The four elements are grouped together under the unifying element which transmutes them all to gold. That is the true function of the Golden Boy as Eternal Youth." Lizzy stopped to take a sip of tea. "Have I missed anything, Septimus?"

"The Golden Boy is meant to represent not only Hermes, but also Hermes Trismegistus, the father of alchemy," Septimus added. "Hidden up there in plain view."

"He's supposed to represent that Hermetic principal 'as above, so below'?" Elizabeth asked.

"Yes, yes. Whatever is manifest on the earthly plain reflects the grater truth in the spiritual plane. Turning the base elements into gold is only the lower manifestation of this. Hermes Trismegistus hoped to teach mankind the greater alchemy. The means by which man could transform himself into the perfection of the gods. The name Eternal Youth was a hint from the creator of the sculpture. 'Immortality', in plainer words." Septimus explained.

"Holy cow, that's a lot to take in. You're saying that the architect took all that into account when he designed the building?" Elizabeth shook her head, trying to get the information to settle into some semblance of order in her mind.

"The important thing, at this moment, is that those stone works will rise to our aid in our hour of need. They will assist me in ensuring your safety as you help Septimus turn the key and seal out the dark for another century," Lizzy replied to her questing glance.

"What key? You still haven't told me exactly what it is I'm supposed to do," Elizabeth dropped back into her chair.

"Whats about us?" Stewart spoke up, wiping cookie crumbs from his chin with the back of his hand.

Elizabeth turned a startled glance his way. She'd totally forgotten the presence of the child spirits.

"It would be best if you two remained here where it is safe," Lizzy said.

"What? And miss all the fun?" Stewart frowned. "We's goin' with ye all. Nothin' ye can do ta stop us, neither."

Septimus sighed. "He's correct, of course. We have no control over the spirits that reside in the building along with us. Perhaps best we keep them close and know where they are, so they don't pop up at the least opportune time."

"I don't like it, but I see your point," Lizzy agreed. She turned a stern gaze on the two spirits. "You will stay with me, no wandering off on your own. Understood?"

Stewart opened his mouth, ready to argue while Sarah peeked out from behind him.

"No more cookies if you don't mind what I say," Lizzy threatened.

Sarah tugged on Stewart's collar until he bent his head down to hers. She whispered something in his ear, her small face screwed up in concentration. Reluctantly, the boy nodded and straightened up.

"Okay, yeah. We'll stick by ye."

"Promise? Do I have your word?" Lizzy prompted.

Stewart hesitated.

"A man is only as good as his word, you know," Septimus reminded him.

Defeated, his shoulders slumped. "Yeah, all right. I gives ye my word." He spit in his palm and offered the hand to Lizzy.

Hiding a smile, Lizzy spit in her palm and clasped the smaller on in hers.

"Seen and acknowledged," Septimus declared. "Now let's get on with this."

"Yes, lets. What key and why the hell is it on the roof?" Elizabeth demanded.

"As I started to explain. We need to be on the roof at the moment the sun breaks the horizon. We will be calling on the power of the sun to seal the dark. One of the ways to call on the sun's power is by the number 666. It is not the number of the devil, or Satan, as some would have you believe. Far further back than that, it was the number of the sun. The architect hinted at that in the dimensions of the Grand Staircase Hall. It measures 66.6 feet on each side of the square, and 666 is a solar invocation. Furthermore, the planets Mercury and Venus, which represent Hermes and Ishtar, were aligned the day the cornerstone was placed in this building. That was not a coincidence, I think."

"Okay, sure. That's cool. But what's the key you keep talking about?" Eizabeth refused to get sidetracked by all the esoteric information.

"Did you know there are two sphinxes on the roof of this building?" Lizzy broke into the conversation.

Elizabeth frowned. "I think I remember reading that somewhere. I remember thinking it was weird. I mean why are there Egyptian lion guys on the roof of the Manitoba legislature building?"

"An excellent question, my dear. There are inscriptions on the breasts of the sphinxes. One of the creatures faces the east and the rising sun, the other faces the west and the setting sun. The north facing Golden Boy overlooks them both from above. With me so far?" Septimus paused.

Elizabeth nodded. "I think so."

"The stone carvings are huge. It is hard to appreciate how large they are without actually standing between their paws. But I assure you, they are far bigger than they appear from the ground. On each sphinx's chest, under the nose and between the giant paws is a flat block of limestone. There are hieroglyphs, symbols, carved on it," Septimus explained.

"You mean like hieroglyphics? Like the Rosetta stone?" Elizabeth interrupted him.

"Somewhat, yes." Septimus nodded.

"Is it written in three languages or just the hieroglyphs?" Elizabeth pressed him. "What does it look like?"

"Just one language. At the top is a circle, below it in a shallow, horizonal rectangle with nine balls on top of it. The last image is a scarab beetle—" Septimus replied.

"Why would someone go to the trouble of providing all that detail when nobody except maybe the pigeons and the odd workman are going to see it. Does it even mean anything?" Elizbeth interrupted him.

"Hey, me and Sarah goes up there in the summer to bring in the longest day. We ain't nobody," Stewart declared, glaring at Elizabeth.

"Sorry, I stand corrected," she apologized with a quick smile. "But what does it mean, if anything?" She turned back to Septimus.

"Of course it means something. Hieroglyphs to some are considered the language of magic. Like a code that could waken the gods. So, let me decipher the images for you. The circle at the top is the sun god Ra. The game board looking thing is pronounced 'men' and means 'everlasting' according to my sources. The scarab is pronounced 'kheper' and means 'manifestation of'. So, if we read them together, the message of the sphinx is this...To read the hieroglyphs as they are supposed to be by an ancient Egyptian you would say 'men kheper Ra' which translates to 'the everlasting manifestation of the sun god Ra'. The three symbols carved in the oval are the throne name of one of the pharaohs.

Thutmosis III, his name in English is 'born of Thut'. He was a great builder of temples. Many Masons and Rosicrucians claim to trace their beginnings back to his mystery school founded in 1489 BCE, which might explain his name being added here. The hieroglyphs outside the oval say: 'the good god gives life'. So, the inscription as a whole, reads 'the everlasting manifestation of the sun god Ra, the good god who gives life'." Septimus leaned back in his seat as he finished.

"All very interesting, I'm sure. But you haven't said anything about this key you keep saying we need to turn," Elizabeth prodded the man.

"The inscription is the key, my dear. I thought you would have figured that out on your own." He closed his eyes and sighed.

"Are you all right?" Lizzy moved to stand beside his chair.

"Yes. Yes, just a bit fatigued. I'll be fine. Don't you worry your head about me." He patted her hand.

"Humph, don't patronize me, old man." Lizzy sniffed hard through her nose. "If you need to rest in order to gather your strength, just say so."

Septimus opened his eyes. "I'm fine, I assure you." He glanced at the clock and got to his feet. "We have time, we should go and ascertain how our allies are faring."

"Yes, of course. You're correct." Lizzy turned to Elizabeth. "Best you wait here.

Septimus and I can move much more freely than you. Being a ghost does have its benefits sometimes." She grinned. "Drink your tea and rest. The night will be through soon enough now."

Elizabeth shrugged. She had no wish to leave the relative sanctuary of the library. Her aches and bruises were making themselves felt. She poured another cup of tea, somehow not surprised the liquid was still boiling hot, and lay back in the chair.

"We can help too." Stewart got to his feet and pulled Sarah up beside him. "We can go check on the others what lives with us. They won't suspect anything iffen we shows up."

"Won't they be suspicious about where you've been while all the fighting has been going on?" Elizabeth asked.

"Nah, I'll jes tell 'em the big black man sent us off on a secret mission, like. Ain't nobody questions anything *he* orders," Stewart said, squaring his shoulders.

"Be off with you, then." Septimus waved them away. "Be back here by four-thirty at the latest. The sun rises at four-fifty-one today. We must be in place before that. If you are waylaid we will not have the time to look for you. At least not until after we perform the ritual."

"We'll be here." Stewart and Sarah winked out of sight before Elizabeth could blink. Somehow, she didn't think she'd ever get used to that.

"We're off too. Mind you stay put, please." Lizzy patted her shoulder. "You're the most important element."

"Why is that? Neither of you has explained that part of this whole thing," Elizabeth asked.

"Oh! No, I suppose we did neglect that little piece of information, didn't we?" Lizzy glanced at Septimus.

"Please accept my apologies, my dear. You are the most important element, because we require the presence, and more importantly the power, of a mortal. As a daughter of Eve, and a direct descendant in the Warwick bloodline, your power is the most potent of all."

"Umm, I see." Elizabeth wasn't quite sure how to process that information. When she looked up, both Septimus and Lizzy had disappeared.

"Great, I'm important because I'm alive. Let's hope that's all there is to it. Nothing like I have to give up my life, or my first born, or something ridiculous like that," she muttered. Her gaze kept drifting to the clock on the wall, where the second hand continued to tick off the moments, unlike her idiot watch that refused to acknowledge that time was indeed passing. Hopefully, once the night was over, and she could return to some semblance of normality, and her watch would co-operate as well. Looking at the wall clock again, she counted down the hours between where the hands stood now at 2:24

am and 7:50 when presumably she was
expected to make her way back up unto that
godforsaken roof. With any luck the blizzard
would have eased up a bit by then. Maybe.

Chapter Eleven

Elizabeth's head jerked forward startling her back to reality. She scrubbed her hands over her face and stood up. "Must have nodded off," she muttered. The hands of the library clock read 2:55 am. Almost three in the morning, still way too much time for her to regret her decision to get mixed up in this craziness. And perhaps the worst part of it was, there was no one, besides her grandmother, she could ever tell about this. Who would believe her even if she tried?

Unable to sit still, she prowled the library, randomly picking books off the shelves and flipping through the pages. To her surprise, the collection included titles in Cree, English, French, Michif, and Ukrainian, along with other languages. She replaced a book back on the shelf and wandered over to one of the tall windows. Pushing the heavy curtain aside, she peered out into the night. The snow whirled against the window; the glass was freezing cold when she pressed her palm on the pane.

The thought of going back up on the roof sent chills down her back. The memory of the sensation of hanging in mid-air just a few hours ago wouldn't leave her mind. If not for her unlikely rescue by the stone statue, she'd be roadkill. Or lawn kill? She shook her head. Didn't matter. Dead was dead. No one could survive the fall from the pediment where the War Chest sat.

Enough of waiting, waiting for someone else to decide what she needed to do. Enough of waiting for things to happen instead of taking action herself. *If I'm so damned important to this mission, or whatever it is, why am I just sitting here doing nothing?*

Spinning away from the window, she crossed the room and pulled the door open. A blast of noise greeted her, and she ducked back a step. The battle was still going on in the rotunda. A soldier of some sort thundered by, clinging to the back of one of the bison/oxen who were chasing down one of the Furies while another Fury swooped down on the pair from above. The Black Star burned with an unearthly light, adding energy to the tornado of darkness that spilled upward out of the marble.

Elizabeth had opened the door with the intention of taking matters into her own hands. The strange creatures and the ferocity of the battle made her rethink that strategy. From what she understood, once the sun rose in the next few hours, all these mythical beings would go back to normal. None of them were in any danger of actually dying. She, on the other hand, could certainly be injured, even killed. She attempted to gauge which way the tide of battle was turning. Were the good guys winning? It was difficult to decide what was what as the battle raged on both the floor of the Black Star and above it in the rotunda.

A Minotaur charged toward where she hovered in the open doorway. The floor shook under his feet. Elizabeth stood mesmerized, her legs refusing to obey the panicked commands from her brain. The wide horns on his bull's head dipped toward her while an eldritch scream rose from his throat. The lowered head rammed itself at the opening; the spread of the horns catching on the frame. The shock of the impact broke the hold of the horror that held Elizabeth immobile. She stumbled backward and slammed the door, forcing the Minotaur out of the way.

Trembling, she fought to control her ragged breathing. The library was a sanctuary, both Lizzy and Septimus agreed on that point. Unless she was foolish enough to venture beyond its borders, she was safe. So much for taking control. She shook her head.

A timid knock sounded on the door. "Let me in. It's me," the voice said.

"Who are you?" Elizabeth moved closer to the door, hand hovering over the handle.

"It's me. Your grandmother. Let me in," the voice cajoled her.

"How do I know it's you?" Elizabeth fought to keep her voice steady.

"Of course it's me, silly girl. Open the door."

Unease shivered over Elizabeth's skin. There was something off about the voice, something a tiny bit alien. Or was it only her paranoia coming to the fore? She dropped her hand and stepped away from the doorway.

"If you're really my grandmother, then you can just pop in here, can't you? You don't need me to open the door," Elizabeth challenged the disembodied voice.

"I can't. I'm hurt. You must let me in." Now the voice was filled with anguish, somehow sounding weaker than it had just a few seconds ago.

"If you're really my grea...." Elizabeth paused. Lizzy wasn't her grandmother; she was her great-grandmother. She backed further away from the door. "I don't believe you! I'll never let you in."

Her words were met with a barrage of frenzied blows that shook the walls, but the door and the protections held firm.

"You will regret denying me! I will flay the skin from your bones while you watch. The fire will take the flesh from your feet as hold them over the red coals." More blows thundered against the door following the threats. Then silence.

She was tempted to peek out the door to see if the owner of the voice was gone, but common sense sent her back to curl up in the armchair. The clock hands stood at 3:15 am.

Time was moving far too slow for her peace of mind, and at the same time, far too fast. While she wanted the others to return in the worst way, she also didn't want to leave the library and return to the roof. "Talk about being stuck between a rock and a hard place," she murmured. "Oh!"

"Sorry, child. Did I startle you?" Gramma Lizzy blinked into view beside Elizabeth's chair.

"Scared the life out of me," she admitted.

Lizzy sank into the chair opposite her, smoothing down the folds of her skirt. "How have things been here? All quiet, I hope."

"Not exactly. One of those guys with the bull's head and the big horns tried to get through the door," Elizabeth told her.

"Oh, my stars. However, did that happen? He shouldn't have been able to open the door." Lizzy caught Elizabeth's gaze.

"Yeah, well...I might have opened the door to see how the battle was going..."

"You foolish child. You could have ruined everything," Lizzy scolded her. "By opening the door, you practically invited him, or something like him, in."

"I didn't know that, did I?" She defended herself. "You guys go off and leave me here all alone. I was curious if our side was winning, and I didn't think it would hurt to have a peek. It's not like you guys are very forthcoming with any information. It's like pulling hen's teeth to get anything out of you."

Lizzy sighed. "You may have a point there. But honestly, we've told you everything you need to know. Some things are unpredictable. The future is fluid, nothing is written in stone, so to speak." She leaned over and squeezed Elizabeth's arm. "It was remiss of us. We should have warned you not to open the door to anyone."

"Yeah, I figured that out. Somebody, or something, was out there pretending to be you, trying to get me to open the door for them—"

"You didn't open it, did you?" Lizzy jumped to her feet, quickly scanning the shadowy shelves rising around them.

"No, of course I didn't. I'm not stupid you know," Elizabeth snapped.

Lizzy sank back into her chair. "No, of course you're not stupid. I never meant to imply that you were. It's just this night is moving along so differently than when I was in your position. It's like the spirit is stronger, as if he's pulling energy from the unrest in the world today. From what I overhear in the Legislature Chamber, the world is a far different place than it was when I was alive."

"I have to agree with you, Gramma Lizzy. The world of politics is very different from a hundred years ago. There's the internet now, and email..."

"I've heard people talk of the internet, but I've never been able to ask someone to explain it properly."

"The internet means that people can access information at any hour of the day or night just by looking at their phone or opening your computer. A person can send a message to someone and get an almost immediate response. It has made the world a much smaller place. That's it in a nutshell," Elizabeth attempted to explain the internet to someone who was only familiar with the early telephone and telegraph systems.

"That sounds fascinating, I'm sure. But perhaps, like the Biblical Tower of Babel, it has a dark side as well," Lizzy mused.

"I'm afraid I have to agree with that," Elizabeth said. She glanced at the clock, it was 3:45. "Shouldn't the others be getting back soon?"

"Yes, I do believe they should be returning in the next few moments." Lizzy got up to brew another pot of tea.

"What did you find out when you were gone? Any sign of the Big Bad?" Elizabeth kept one eye on the clock. There was no reason to keep looking at the door when the ones she was expecting would just appear at some point.

"The battle goes on. We're neither winning nor losing, but the activity is keeping The Abiff's supporters from causing more trouble." Lizzy slipped a quilted tea cozy over the steaming pot, setting it down on the side table with the cups and saucers.

"We're back, missus." Stewart and then Sarah winked into existence. '

"Is there any cocoa?" Sarah stared hopefully at Lizzy.

"And cookies?" Stewart chimed in.

"I'll see what I can find." Lizzy smiled at the two spirits and disappeared behind a shelf of books. She emerged moments later with a plate of cookies and a cobalt blue chocolate pot balanced on a round china tray. "Here we are."

Stewart and Sarah wiggled into one of the armchairs together, faces turned expectantly toward the older woman. Soon they were holding tiny cups of chocolate and a plate of cookies rested on the table beside them.

"Thankee, missus." Stewart sprayed crumbs down his shirt, laughter dancing in his eyes. Sarah smiled, her mouth too full for words.

"We didn't find nothin'. Looks like them weird critters are all in the round room. Couldn't find hide ner hair of 'em anywheres else," Stewart reported.

"Did you see Septimus in your travels?" Elizabeth queried.

"Nope. Didn' see Septi anywheres we was, did we Sarie."

Sarah shook her head in agreement. "Didn' see 'em," she confirmed.

"Well, I'm confident he will show up before we need to carry on." Lizzy's tone was confident, but a small furrow of worry creased her forehead.

"What do we do if he's held up?" Elizabeth wondered. "Can we do what needs to be done without him?"

"It would be best if Septimus was present. He is the other side of the cipher, if you will. The mortal, that's you Elizabeth, and the immortal, that's Septimus. I'm not sure what would happen if one or the other was missing," Lizzy admitted.

"Great. Does The Abiff guy know that? If he does, all he has to do to win is, at the very least, delay Septimus, or worst case scenario, get rid of him somehow." Elizabeth caught her bottom lip in her teeth.

"Now, now. Let's not go borrowing trouble, shall we?" Lizzy cautioned. "As I said, I have every confidence in the man's ability to take care of himself. He'll be here." She threw a surreptitious glance at the clock.

Elizabeth noted that the hands now stood at 8:05 am. She sank deeper in her chair and nursed the cup of tea Lizzy handed her. There was no point in worrying. The events were out of her hands now and what would come would come. A sense of peace settled over her, she was somehow detached from what was happening around her, almost displaced. Maybe she'd been away from her own time and reality for too long, the thought floated through her mind and was quickly dismissed. She existed in a bubble, separate from the spirits who inhabited the space with her. Perhaps it was her humanity that set her apart, or perhaps the blood pumping in her veins and the ability to die. She tipped her head back and closed her eyes.

* * *

"Oh, thank goodness!"

Lizzy's exclamation startled Elizabeth, she jumped and splashed tepid tea onto her lap. Righting the cup and saucer and placing it on the table, she got to her feet. Septimus stood behind Stewart and Sarah, leaning on the back of their armchair. His top hat appeared a tad crumpled and his neck cloth askew.

"Gracious, what happened to you?" Lizzy hurried to his side, taking his arm and settling him in the chair she just vacated.

"It's nothing to worry yourself about." He waved his hand, though he leaned his head wearily on the back of the chair.

"Now, now. Here drink this, it will make you feel better." Lizzy pressed a cup of hot, heavily sugared tea into his hand.

Elizabeth knelt beside him, warily watching to see if she needed to rescue the tea from his shaking hand. "Are you sure you're okay? What happened?"

Septimus raised the cup to his mouth, only spilling a bit into the saucer in the process. "Just a spot of trouble. It's all taken care of for the moment. Ah, yes, that's capital. Much better. My thanks, Lizzy." He finished the tea and set the cup and saucer down on the table beside him.

"Fine, now tell us what went on," Lizzy demanded. "We were starting to worry."

"As I said, there was a spot of trouble. I came upon The Abiff unexpectedly, and I'm afraid I have to confess that I was less than prepared for the encounter."

"Oh, my." Lizzy let her breath out in a huff.

"He held me up for longer than I would have liked, but it all came right in the end." He paused. "At least for now."

"What does that mean?" Elizabeth went back to her chair and perched on the edge, elbow resting on her knees.

Septimus sighed. "It means that the encounter took more out of me than I anticipated."

"But, you'll be okay, right? Ready to go up on the roof and do whatever it is we're supposed to do?" Elizabeth frowned.

"Yes, I'll be fine. Perhaps another cup of tea would be in order?" He raised an eyebrow at Lizzy. "After that I shall be ready to do battle once more."

"Here you are, my dear." Lizzy filled his cup from the teapot she kept at her side.

Steam rose in fragrant streams from the golden liquid.

"Just the thing." Septimus smiled at her and brought the cup to his lips.

Elizabeth checked the time on the library clock. The hands stood at 8:15 am. Reluctantly, she brought her attention back to Septimus. "It's almost four-thirty. We need to go soon, don't we?"

"Yes, yes. I suppose we do." He set the cup and saucer down and made an attempt to straighten his neckcloth. "Are you ready?" Septimus asked Lizzy.

"As ever," she replied. "What are we to do with Stewart and Sarah?"

"We ain't stayin' here alone!" Stewart leaped to his feet, pulling Sarah up to stand beside him. "We's goin' with you. Ain't we Sarah?"

The small spirit nodded, her tangled hair bouncing on her thin shoulders. "Goin' with you," she confirmed.

"Will they be safe?" Elizabeth looked to Septimus and Lizzy for the answer.

"As safe as anywhere, I suppose." Lizzy didn't sound confident, and her expression revealed her misgivings. She turned to the two small spirits. "You must agree to obey me and do whatever I say. No questions, no arguments. Is that understood?"

Stewart and Sarah nodded, their faces serious and solemn.

"If one of us tells you to disappear, you must do so immediately. There is no time for hesitation in the heat of the moment." Septimus fixed them both with a gimlet stare.

"Understood." Stewart spoke for both of them.

"Fine. Then here is what we will do. We will all proceed to the sphinxes using the same staircase as before. Elizabeth, you will go to the sphinx that faces the dawn in the east, I will take my place at the one in the west, where the sun disappears at night. That is important, so we must not get confused, no matter what happens. Understood?"

"Yes, I go to the one in the east. Which way should I turn when we come out of the staircase? Just in case I get confused which way is east when we get up there." Elizabeth wanted to be sure she didn't screw up.

"When we emerge, you should turn to your left. No matter what. I have no idea if The Abiff will have any surprises for us, or one of his minions, for that matter." Septimus frowned.

"Okay. Got it. Turn left until I run into the sphinx." Elizabeth nodded.

"Lizzy, you will stay near the staircase door and guard it. The little ones should stay with you, then if need be they can escape without any trouble. It will be your responsibility to alert us if there is any danger, other than the ones we already are aware of," Septimus instructed.

"Is it still storming out there?" Elizabeth looked at the tall windows which were encrusted with snow so that she couldn't see out of them.

"Yes, I imagine the blizzard will continue as we work. However, if I can manage it, I will do my best to manifest a protective bubble around us. That was the original plan, but my little encounter with our enemy has sapped some of my powers," Septimus admitted.

"That would be nice, if you can manage it," Elizabeth said. "So, once I get out there and find the lion guy, what am I supposed to do? And when?"

"Ah, yes. The time has come to reveal that information." Septimus got to his feet and glanced at the clock. "Excellent, we have time to go over it here, before we leave for the roof." The clock hands stood at 8:19am. "Now, as you may recall, there are symbols carved on the lozenge on the lion's chest." He looked to Elizabeth for her confirmation. Receiving it, he continued. "Excellent. Once we are both in place, Lizzy will wave a red scarf when it is five minutes to sun rise. That should occur at eight-twenty-four this morning. At her signal, we will both start to trace the symbols with our right forefinger. Starting with the bar with the dots above it in the centre of the middle oval. As you do that you say 'men', then move on to the scarab and as you trace that symbol you say 'khper' then move to the circle at the top of the oval and as you trace that, you say 'Ra'. Count to three and then say 'the everlasting manifestation of the sun god Ra' which is the English version of the invocation. Wait three seconds after you finish. Next, trace the symbols outside the oval, starting with the one in the top left that looks like an upside down hurly stick, as you complete the tracing say 'the good' then move on to the one on the other side of the lozenge, trace it and say 'god' before proceeding to the lower ones. Again, starting on the lefthand side. Trace the double triangle, saying 'who gives' as you finish, then trace the ankh symbol saying 'life' as you finish. When you have traced all four symbols, put both hands on the lozenge, trust your instincts as to where to place them, turn your face to the east and repeat the invocation is as loud a voice as you can. If I can manage the bubble of protection, you should be able to hear me doing the same thing. Hopefully, together, we will chant the final invocation. "The everlasting manifestation of the sun god Re, the good god who gives life". Do you need to write any of that down? It is imperative that you get the words correct. That is more important than the timing, but the timing is also important, so don't hesitate." Septimus glanced at the clock. "It is time."

Gathering the child spirits before him, Septimus led the way out of the library into the relative calm of the outer area. The combatants seemed to have gone elsewhere, much to Elizabeth's relief. She trailed behind the tall man and the children with Lizzy bringing up the rear. They reached the camouflaged entrance to the narrow stairway without any interference. Elizabeth ducked her head as she entered, the low ceiling evoking an unfamiliar sense of claustrophobia. Nerves, she thought. I've never had any issue with small spaces before. You've never done battle with some crazy mythical beings before either, she reminded herself.

The steep climb sent knives of pain in her calves and thighs, but she pressed on, using the discomfort to distract her from worrying about what might lie ahead at the top of the steps. She bumped into Septimus when he halted on the narrow landing, the child spirits huddled beside him. He held up his hand for silence and slipped the door open a crack.

"All clear," he whispered.

A lash of cold air and snow blew through the opening. Elizabeth shivered and wished she'd thought to borrow a sweater from Lizzy, then realized how foolish that sounded. She followed the tall man out onto the roof, Lizzy holding Stewart and Sarah with her in the doorway. Blinding sheets of white whipped cross the exposed area, tall curtains of whirling snow threw icy bits biting into Elizabeth's face. Her hair tore free of the pins which held it, and long curls whipped about her head. Cold fingers fumbled to untie the silk scarf from around her neck, once she managed to free it, she tied it over her hair, fighting the wind that threatened to snatch it from her hands.

With her hair confined, her vision was still shrouded by the storm. She grabbed Septimus' hand to catch his attention. Leaning close she shouted in his ear. "Can you do anything about the wind?"

"A moment, child. I just need to catch my breath for a moment." He turned from her and raised his hands toward the sky, head tipped back staring upward, his lips moving soundlessly.

Elizabeth stepped back, wrapping her arms around her waist. She checked where she was relative to the stairway door, then peered through the snow in the direction she guessed the sphinx should be. "Left of the door," she muttered. "Now all I have to do is reach the darn thing and not fall off the roof in the process." The blast of wind disappeared so quickly Elizabeth stumbled and braced a hand on the wall for support. She wiped the wet from her face and turned to Septimus.

"Better?" He grinned at her and straightened his top hat.

"Much." Elizabeth grinned back.

"Let's get on with this before we have company." Septimus gestured toward the stone sphinxes which were now protected by the bubble he had created. Outside of the confines the prairie blizzard raged, coating the transparent membrane with ice.

"Is it time to start?" Elizabeth wanted to be sure she didn't mess anything up by starting the invocation too soon, or too late."

"Yes. It is time. We should finish right on schedule with the rise of the sun. You remember the words and the order you say them in?" Septimus regarded her for a long moment.

"I got it." Elizabeth nodded. "I won't forget any of it."

"Excellent." Septimus turned toward Lizzy and the child spirits. "If any unwelcome company should show up, shout a warning, but don't endanger yourselves."

"You worry about what you need to do and let me worry about my part, old friend. I know my duty as well as you know yours." Lizzy sniffed and looked down her nose at him, a hand resting on each of the little spirits' heads.

Septimus shook his head. Elizabeth didn't think he agreed with Lizzy at all. But time was moving on and there was a job to do. She stepped carefully across the snowy footing and edged around the sphinx's paw which towered over her head. Not having been as close to the statues as this, she'd not realized just how huge they were. Standing in the empty space between the front legs she looked up at the engraved lozenge. It would be a stretch to reach the top symbols but after careful consideration, she decided she could manage. Unable to see Lizzy, Elizabeth peered around the paw closest to the doorway in time to see Lizzy give her the signal to begin. The red scarf billowed in her hand and Elizabeth waved in response. She darted a glance across to Septimus and he waved her back to her place. Satisfied that they were on schedule, Elizabeth took a deep breath, took a moment to run through the order in her mind and then set her right forefinger on the dotted bar in the middle of the oval. Initially, the stone was cold enough to burn her flesh, but as she moved across the image and uttered the word 'men', the stone warmed. She moved on to the scarab beetle, the stone growing warmer as she followed the inscription, intoning 'khper' as she did so. *I hope I said that right.* Her concentration slipped for a second. Refocusing, she moved to the circle at the top of the oval drawing her finger around the edge and repeating the words Septimus gave her: 'Ra'. She counted to three and intoned 'the everlasting manifestation of the sun god Ra' as she'd been instructed.

Elizabeth let out the breath she'd been holding and moved on to the next bit. Standing on her toes, she waited another three seconds before putting her finger on the top left symbol. The stone was more than pleasantly warm now. She outlined the symbol, intoning 'the good' as she finished and moved on to the one on the other side of the lozenge. She followed the outline of the symbol that resembled some kind of ancient stringed instrument, at least to her mind. "God," she whispered as she completed the gesture. The stone was hot now, burning through her clothes as she leaned on the sphinx to reach the image.

She slid down the sphinx to reach the lower images. Under her fingers the double triangle in the lower left hand corner shone with a red glow. When she put her finger on it, the image was hot but not too uncomfortable. Her finger seemed to move of its own accord, following the double lines. "Who gives," she whispered, her finger completing the last stroke. She shuffled across between the paws and came to the last symbol. Holding her breath, she drew her finger around the familiar form of the ankh. "Life," she whispered.

The stone was glowing now, the whole statue flaming with gold and red ripples. The last thing Elizabeth wanted to do was touch the darn thing. What if it came to life and decided it didn't like the tiny mortal trapped between its paws? Nonsense, commonsense said, but after the craziness of the night, Elizabeth wasn't sure she could currently delineate the non from the common.

"Now! Elizabeth! Now!" Septimus' voice spurred her on, compelling her to finish what they had started.

Biting her lip, she reached out with both hands for the brilliantly glowing lozenge, the symbols blazing with white blossoms of fire.

Her hands disappeared into the flames up to her wrists, surprised they didn't burn to a crisp, Elizabeth leaned closer. She glanced toward Septimus to see him enveloped in golden-white light. He nodded at her and turned his face to the west. Remembering the rest of her instructions, Elizabeth turned toward the east.

"Now, together," Septimus called.

Her voice rang out, perfecting in sync with his. "The everlasting manifestation of the sun god Ra..." Both voices faltered at the same time. The protective bubble evaporated in an instant; snow blew into Elizabeth's face, and she could no longer see or hear Septimus. The sphinx continued to glow and flare under her touch, unhindered by the sudden blast of cold. She huddled closer to it while invisible hands gripped her shoulders and attempted to pry her away from the statue. *What is going on?* Without removing her hands from the stone, she tried to see Lizzy, but the lion's leg was too high. It must be The Abiff, or some of his allies. The panicked thought reverberated in her head. *I need to finish the invocation. Don't know if it will do any good if Septimus can't finish his part, but I need to do this.* Elizabeth pressed her body against the lozenge.

"Let go of me!" she shrieked when hands gripped her upper arms and attempted to lift her away. Somehow the light held her steady, even as her hands began to slip away from the stone.

"Arghhhhh," a voice screeched over the howl of the wind. The hands clutching Elizabeth vanished.

"That'll teach 'em," Stewart stood at her side, wiping his hands on his trousers. "Go on, then. Ye gotta finish them fancy words like yon Septi." He nodded toward where she supposed the other sphinx stood obscured by the blizzard.

A thousand voices filled the air with shrieks and curses overpowering the scream of the wind. Elizabeth's courage shrank into a hard nut in her stomach, her fingers starting to slide off the stone. Would this night never end? Where was the sun? Even if it did rise, who would know in this storm?

"Do it!" Stewart poked her hard in the ribs. "Ye gotta. An' don' fergit ye promised to help me and Sarie move on. Do it. Now!"

Fighting down her panic, Elizabeth ignored the unearthly, eldritch screams. Pressing her hands firmly onto the stone, unflinching when the flames reached her shoulders and then covered her with light. She had no idea what, or if, Septimus was saying, but she would do her part.

"The everlasting manifestation of the sun god Ra, the good god who gives life." She repeated it three times, even though Septimus hadn't told her to do so. Her grandmother always said three was a sacred number, saying something three times in a row made it stronger so it would carry more magic. Elizabeth had forgotten that bit of advice until just this minute and figured it couldn't hurt.

The light surrounding the sphinx exploded in a rainbow of colour, every colour of the rainbow and colours Elizabeth had never seen before. Colours she was fairly sure didn't exist in the mundane world as she formerly knew it. Music flared, horns and flutes, stringed instruments, the deep notes of cello being carried higher by the delicate notes of the viola. The sharp clang of cymbals. Over and around her, thrumming through her until her very bones vibrated with the glory of the music. 'I am the foundation of creation', it sang to her. 'Music underpins all things; it is the bones of all that is. Music creates the mathematical matrix that holds the world together. Know this and remember.' She gave herself up to the magic and wonder, nothing existed but the music and her spirit. Elizabeth soared on the symphony of sound, disembodied and following the splashes of colour awoken by the music as it climbed higher before swooping down into the lower registers.

Gradually, the music became fainter. Elizabeth tried to capture the last strains, clutch them to her, reluctant to release their hold on her. Her vision, which had been blinded by the light, grew grey at the edges before resolving back to normal. Her spirit settled back into her corporeal body with a sigh.

She looked to the east, but there was nothing to see but clouds and snow. In her heart of hearts though, Elizabeth knew the sun had broken the horizon, unseen in the blizzard's blanket. She leaned her forehead on the sphinx's chest. To her surprise, warm fur tickled her nose. Her head popped up and she found herself looking into the liquid amber eyes of the pharaoh. "How..."

"Well done, daughter of Eve. The dark is banished once more. Until we meet again, The Elizabeth." His words vibrated in her chest, melodious and sweet, yet as deep as the granite bones of the earth. Even as she gazed up at him, the mobile flesh solidified, the warm fur under her fingers transmogrifying back to stone. Elizabeth stood still, reluctant to break the tenuous contact she still felt with the creature.

"C'mon. Let's go. The others are waitin'." Stewart poked her in the ribs again.

Elizabeth let her fingers glide down the lozenge before stepping away. After one last look upward, she skirted the lion's paw and made her way toward the doorway where Lizzy and Sarah waited. Septimus limped into view from the far side of the west sphinx.

"Did we do it?" Elizabeth called to him.

"What do you think?" Septimus' reply was tinged with exhaustion. "Did you not experience the glory? If we had not been successful, the light would not have bloomed, the music would not have caught you up in its crescendo."

"Sorry I asked," she muttered.

"Don't ask foolish questions you already know the answers to." Septimus hobbled to her side.

"Septimus," Lizzy's voice held a warning note.

He raised his head and gave the older woman a faint smile. "Yes, you're correct. I should not take out my exhaustion on someone else." He turned to Elizabeth and sketched a shallow bow. "Please accept my apologies, Elizabeth. The battle has taken more out of me than I realized."

"Sure. Apology accepted." Elizabeth shrugged. "Are you sure you're okay?" She moved to take the tall man by the arm.

"Nothing a good cuppa won't cure," he assured her.

"Come then. Let's get off this roof and back to the library." Lizzy herded them into the narrow confines of the staircase. "The longest night is over, and we have emerged victorious. We all deserve a nice hot cup of tea with lots of sugar."

Elizabeth trailed at the end of the company; an echo of the glorious music held close to her heart. *Well, we made it through the night. Now what happens?* She was glad to reach the end of the steep stairway and step out into the hallway. It was still very early in the morning, no one was likely to be about. Not even the security team. *Not with this weather. The city must be shut down with all this snow. When I find my phone I need to call Gramma and let her know I'm okay. She'll never believe what I have to tell her about what's happened. Or maybe she will....*

Chapter Twelve

In a daze of weariness Elizabeth followed Lizzy along the dimly lit hall to the library. She skirted the debris left from the battle scattered across the marble floors. Reaching the undisturbed sanctuary of the library, Elizabeth sank into one of the armchairs. Septimus collapsed into the one across from her. In less time than seemed possible, Lizzy produced a pot of steaming tea and a plate of biscuits. Stewart and Sarah sat cross-legged on the carpet at Lizzy's feet.

Septimus accepted the cup and saucer from Lizzy and took a long drink. He raised his head and looked across at the librarian. "Someone should go and check that The Abiff has gone back into the abyss. Ensure that the rotunda and the Pool of the Black Star are restored to their neutral state and the portal is indeed closed."

"Of course. Just to be certain." Lizzy frowned at him with narrowed eyes. "You don't have any suspicions that something is amiss, do you?" She set her cup down and rose to her feet.

"I'll go, missus," Stewart offered, cramming the last of a cookie into his mouth. He got to his feet and patted Sarah on the head. "You wait here. No need both of us goin'." He winked out of sight with a whisper of displaced air.

Elizabeth shook her head. *When something like that seems commonplace I think I need a vacation.* Stewart's reappearance didn't even make her flinch a tiny bit. *Yup, I'm officially crazy. Ghosts and spirits and insane Greek and Roman gods and goddesses, Furies and Gorgons and, God help me, Minotaurs. And I can't even share this with my friends, just Gramma. They'd lock me up in the psych ward at Health Sciences if I breathed a word of this.*

"All good," Stewart announced, slapping his hands together. "All them weird beasties is gone. Them buffalo were just headin' back to where they's supposed to be."

"What about Athena and Medusa—" Septimus began.

"Present and accounted for." Athena stepped into the room without bothering to open the door. Medusa appeared behind the other goddess, her hair hissing softly and twisting about her shoulders.

"I do wish you'd not do that," Lizzy indicated the closed door they'd just walked through. "It is considered polite to announce your presence before your arrival."

Medusa snorted, snakes framing her face raising their heads, tongues flickering toward Lizzy. Athena deigned to reply, just stared down her aristocratic nose at the librarian.

"Manner aside, we are most grateful for your assistance," Septimus broke the sibilant silence. He waved a hand at the hissing serpents who subsided into the tangle on Medusa's head. "Have the others returned to their places already?"

"Mostly," Medusa replied. "There might be a few stragglers still roaming about, but for the most part things have gone back to what might be considered normal."

Athena cleared her throat and glanced at her counterpart. "I suppose we should leave as well." She sighed and shuffled her feet. "I must say I'm not looking forward to another century of hanging about in the Grand Staircase being forced to listen to the inane squabbling of the mortals."

"I understand and I sympathise, but there does not seem to be a viable alternative." Septimus spread his hands and shrugged.

"*Le luppiter dique omnes perdant!*" Medusa cursed. "One day we will find a way to divest our spirits of this infernal clay and walk the earth again to be worshiped by mortals.

Lizzy smothered a giggle and set her cup down. "I doubt very much that Jupiter and all the gods care enough about our situation to damn anyone."

"*I in malam crucem,*" Medusa muttered, setting her serpents to hissing once again.

"Now, now. There's no need for anyone to go and get hanged," Septimus interceded.

"I, myself, must also retire to the shadows once all is concluded." He sighed. "I confess, it is not something I relish either."

"It was a privilege to do battle in your company," Athena spoke, giving a slight bow. "Come along, my dear. It is time we should be back at our places and take up the guardianship with which we are charged."

Medusa muttered something too low for Elizabeth to make out, but from the mutinous expression on her face, she could only surmise it wasn't polite. The goddess took a reluctant step toward the door.

Athena followed, giving Medusa a shove between the shoulder blades as they neared the door. "*Amove te*," she said with laughter bubbling in her voice. "Get out."

Elizabeth watched them flow through the solid door and shook her head. She set her teacup down and got to her feet. "I should go and see what damage there is out there. I really don't know how I'm going to explain all the broken statuary and the other mess." She sank back into her chair and put her hands over her face. "I'm going to get fired for sure. When they figure out that I was the only one here all night and then they see...that..." She waved a hand in the direction of the rotunda and other areas where the battles had raged. "And the portraits...Oh God...if those priceless portraits are destroyed, or even damaged, Oh God. I'm going to jail, let alone losing my job."

"Now, child. Things are not quite that dire." Lizzy patted her bent head. "Why don't you and I go for a stroll and see what can be done about the destruction."

"I don't think I want to see." Elizabeth fought back tears. "There's no way I could get it all cleared up before someone manages to get through the snow and shows up here."

"Come along, now. Perhaps things are not quite as calamitous as you imagine." Lizzy took her great granddaughter's hand and pulled her to her feet.

Elizabeth allowed herself to be removed from her chair and followed Lizzy across the room. "We're opening the door, right?" She hesitated, unwilling to be towed *through* the door.

Lizzy laughed and pulled the door open. They stepped out into the lobby and moved toward the wide stairs. The bison were back in place and looked like ordinary bison now. No trace of their oxen otherness that had manifested itself during the long night. Elizabeth paused as they passed them, tipping her head back, she walked over to the one on the left, reaching out to touch the bronze that still held a trace of warmth. She rejoined Lizzy at the bottom of the flight of stairs.

"It was all real, wasn't it? I'm not having some weird hallucination, am I?" Elizabeth tipped her head to the side. The woman beside her seemed solid enough, the sleeve smooth where her hand rested on Lizzy's jacket.

"Yes, my dear. It was real. You must try to remember as much as you can. Once things go back to the way they were, write it all down in a journal." Lizzy smiled at her.

"Remember? I'm not likely to forget," Elizabeth exclaimed.

"You'd be surprised. As time goes on, it is only natural for the mortal mind to reject that which it does not really understand. Take my advice, please. Write it down while it is still fresh and has not faded in the light of your reality. It is important."

"Okay, I guess I can see where you're going with that. I'll record it all as soon as I get back to my office. Buy why is it so important to remember every little detail? It's not like I can every share it with anyone."

"Oh, but you will." Lizzy started up the steps. "Share it, I mean."

"With who?" Elizabeth laughed at the idea of trying to explain anything about last night.

"With your daughter, when it is time to pass on the legacy." Lizzy's firm tone defied any resistance.

"My daughter? I'm not even married yet." She hurried to come even with the librarian.

"You will be married, and you will have a daughter, mayhap more than one."

"Okay, sure. I'm not going to argue with you about that. But if I have daughters, plural, how will I know which ones gets the unenviable honour of receiving the information?"

"You will just know. I can't explain it, but trust me, your instincts will not lead you astray," Lizzy assured her. "And when your daughter has a daughter, or daughters, she too, in her time, will know which girl will carry on the legacy."

"Lucky kid," her tone was laced with sarcasm. She took the last step and stopped dead at the top of the stairs.

The room lay quiet and serene before her. The centre of the balustrade was bathed in pale golden light, the maleficent black tornado gone without a trace. Elizabeth rushed over to the balustrade and peered down into the Pool of the Black Star. The eight-pointed star lay where it always had. The veined marble shimmering, the image of the star following her as she moved around the opening.

"What happened to all the mess?" Elizabeth turned to Lizzy. "Who cleaned it all up?"

Lizzy smiled. Once The Abiff was sent back to the abyss, the veil between the worlds snapped shut again. The world you are familiar with took precedence once more," she explained.

"You mean I was moving in two planes of existence at once? How is that even possible?" Elizabeth gripped the railing to stave off the wave of fatigue and dizziness that swept over her.

"No. Not exactly..." the librarian hesitated.

"How, not exactly?" Elizabeth wasn't sure she wanted to hear the answer.

"By the paradox that exists between planes, your corporeal body can stay on plane while your spirit body can travel to others simultaneously."

"But this body, right now, feels real. It's physical, I can feel pain, so how can it just be a spirit body?" Elizabeth argued.

"We are special, you and me. As are our descendants who will carry on the legacy. We have the ability to manifest corporally in more than one plane." Lizzy shrugged. "Since I am now deceased in your reality, I only exist in this plane that we presently inhabit. You, however, are both here and still in your office."

"Huh. I'm not sure I'm okay with that, but it seems there isn't anything I can do about it at this point." Elizabeth frowned. "You're telling me I'm still in my office...what...asleep?"

"That is how it will appear to anyone who happens to come across you while you are still in this plane, yes." Lizzy nodded.

"Huh," Elizabeth repeated. Walking around the rotunda, she examined the stonework that only hours before had been splintered and damaged. It now appeared as if there had never been a fierce battle within the walls. "The whole place is back to normal? I won't have to explain anything?"

"That is so." Lizzy agreed. "Now, shall we retire to the library? There are a few items that need attending to before the spell of the longest night is lifted and time moves forward once more."

With a last glance over her shoulder, to assure herself everything was indeed in order, Elizabeth followed the tall woman back to the library where Septimus and the child spirits waited. Entering the room, she reclaimed her armchair and turned to Septimus.

"What happens now? Do you just, I don't know…disappear? Go back to wherever it is you came from? And Gramma Lizzy?"

"In the next little while, the blizzard will ease off. The winds will drop, and the city will start to come alive again. Here, in this building, I will stay as I am, existing on this plane that is one step removed from the world that you know. Lizzy will resume her duties in the library, also in this plane," he explained.

"Will I be able to see you both sometimes? I know there's always rumours going around about the night security guards seeing a lady in the reading room stacking files or replacing books on the shelves. That's you, isn't it?" Elizabeth looked over at Lizzy.

She nodded. "It's me, yes. Some people are more sensitive to the vibrations of the other planes than others. They often catch glimpses of me. It is most prevalent on the gateway days of the year."

"Like the solstices and the equinoxes? What about the cross-quarter days, Imbolc, Beltainne, Lughnasadh and Samhain?" Elizabeth wanted the days clear in her mind.

"Most often on the quarter days, which as you know are the solstices and equinoxes. However, the fire festival days are also when there is a thinning of the veils, especially at Samhain, which the Christians call All Hallows Eve. At those times it is easiest for those who are sensitive to accidentally catch sight of spirits." Septimus clarified for her.

"And if I made the effort to actually seek you guys out, one of those days would be the best time?" Elizabeth asked. "I can't imagine never seeing or talking to you again."

"It will be easiest on those days, but now that we have done battle together, all you need do is quiet your mind and call me. The rotunda or the Pool of the Black Star are the best places to make that call," Septimus replied.

"And you, Gramma Lizzy?" She touched the other woman's arm. "I feel so close to you now, I don't want to lose that connection." A thought occurred to her. "My gramma is your daughter, could she come with me and see you as well?"

Gramma Lizzy's expression was uncertain. "Like Septimus, I will always be available to you when you call. For Liza...I'm not sure, but oh, it would be wonderful to see her again. See the woman she has grown into. Perhaps once this is all neatly tied up, you could bring her here at Imbolc and see what happens." Her face shone with excitement. "Oh, that would be so wonderful."

"I agree. I'll talk to Gramma about when I get home. I bet she'll be up for it." Elizabeth clapped her hands.

"Time grows short. There is one more thing that needs to be done," Septimus declared.

"Yeah, what about us, missus?" Stewart shoved his way into the conversation. "Ye made us a promise and I means to see that ye keep it."

"I haven't forgotten. I'm just not sure how to go about opening the gate, or portal, or whatever it is I need to do to let you both move on," Elizabeth said. "Any idea?" She turned to Septimus and Lizzy.

"Septi, ye must know the secret, dontcha?" Stewart tugged on the man's sleeve.

"I don' wants to stay here anymore. I wanna see my ma again, and my da," Sarah pleaded, eyes shiny with tears. "Ye promised, you gotta keep yer promises."

"I promised I would do my best to help you. That's all I can do. Now let me think on this for a moment and talk to Septimus and Lizzy." Elizabeth drew the two away from the children. "I did promise, I'm just not sure what to do."

"I think the most important thing is what the children themselves wish to have happen," Lizzy mused. "If they truly wish to move on to the next plane, to join their loved ones, then they are actually the ones whose need will open the portal."

"I believe Lizzy has the right of it," Septimus agreed. "What we need to do is offer them the support they require. To steady them if they waver; moving on sounds easy, and in a way it is, but it can also be daunting to leave what is familiar and known and step into that which is unknown. They are only children after all, regardless of how many years they have been trapped here."

"Let me get this straight before I go and talk to them. We need Stewart and Sarah to concentrate on where they want to go, who they want to find on the other side, then we hold space for them, keep them protected while they make the transition," Elizabeth laid it out so that it made sense to her.

"Precisely. And we encourage them if something frightens them. The most important thing is they keep their destination firmly in their mind," Septimus said.

"Ready?" Gramma Lizzy asked.

Elizabeth nodded. "I think so. I'll go talk to them now. Should we do it here in the library or in the basement where they usually hide?"

"Here I think. There are other child spirits in the basement who are ill-disposed to those wishing to move on," Septimus advised.

"That is true," Lizzy agreed. "Here it is then."

Elizabeth went and knelt by the chair where the two child spirits were curled up. "Are you very sure this is what you want?" She laid a hand on each of them. "You have to be very sure you want to move on to the next plane."

Both heads nodded. Sarah had her hand clutched tightly with Stewart's. "I'm sure," she whispered. "I wants ta see my ma, and my da." Her bottom lip trembled.

"Stewart?" Elizabeth prompted.

"Yeah, I wanna see my pa. I don' like it here, never have. But I couldn't never figger out how to git a' here." His gaze held Elizabeth's as he spoke.

"All right, then. Here's what I need you to do. Concentrate really hard on the people you want to see. If you don't remember what they look like, then think about how you feel when you think about them, any memories of how they felt when you were with them. Can you do that?" Elizabeth sat back on her heels.

"I reckon I can," Stewart said. He put an arm around Sarah. "We're gonna go to the same place, right?"

"I hope so. If that's what both of you really want, then I think that is what will happen," Elizabeth said, and hoped it was so.

"I don' wanna go somewheres wifout Stewart," Sarah confided.

"Okay, then. Both of you hold on to the connection you have with each other, when you're thinking about where you want to go, be sure to think about both of you being there. Ready?" Elizabeth looked at Septimus for his agreement. He nodded at her to continue.

"Are you both thinking of those people you love and want to be with? Let me know when you're certain you have them clear in your mind." Elizabeth held her breath and waited while the child spirits' faces scrunched up with concentration. The seconds ticked by in time with her heartbeat. *Dear God, let me be doing the right thing. Don't let me screw this up and make it worse for them.* She crossed her fingers inside her pocket.

"We's ready," Stewart broke the silence.

"I believe you are," Gramma Lizzy whispered, gesturing to the oval of glowing golden light forming before the chair.

"Think really hard," Elizabeth coached them. "Look into the light and see your loved ones waiting for you."

The oval expanded, reaching toward the edges of the armchair. Faint music floated into the room. Elizabeth tipped her head to one side. A nursery song, an old one her gramma used to sing to her. The light became more silver than gold, tendrils reaching out toward the two children. More music, different music, an accordion, a fiddle, happy music. It grew louder as the light increased. A warm breeze lifted the hair on Elizabeth's head. She resisted the urge to reach out and run her fingers through that wonderous illumination.

"Ma?" Sarah reached out her hand and a tendril of light wrapped around it. "Ma? Da?"

"Wait fer me," Stewart cried, reaching out his hand toward the clearing that was opening in the midst of the glowing oval. "I can see my pa, he's playing his fiddle and me auntie is dancing the jig." Wonder filled his voice. "Pa!" The joyful music swelled to a pitch, the light danced to the tune and colours swirled around the room, before concentrating on the two figures in the chair.

"Oh my," Elizabeth whispered. A woman in rough homespun clothing appeared in the wavering light in the middle of the oval.

"Come home now, children. It's been a long time that we've been waiting for you," the woman's voice mixed with the music. "Come home to those who love you."

Stewart and Sarah stood and moved toward the woman. "Ma!" Sarah cried throwing herself at the woman. She held out her hand to Stewart who hesitated, looking back at Septimus.

"Boyo, shake a leg, time's a'wastin'," a man with a fiddle in his hand stepped out of the portal, reaching his free hand toward Stewart. "It's goin' to be late for the *cèilidh*, ye'll be, and we're sure to have lots of craic. Come along, lad."

"Pa!" Stewart lunged toward the man, burying his face in the man's shirt. The man's arms closed around him.

The two children turned and gripped their hands together. Sarah's mother inclined her head toward Elizabeth and smiled while stroking her daughter's hair. "You have my thanks and my blessing."

Stewart's father raised cornflower blue eyes to her and gave her a saucy wink. "It's me thanks ye'll be havin' too fer seein' me boy safely home."

Elizabeth found she couldn't get words past the lump in her throat. The music flared again as the light intensified and the clear portal began to fade. She raised her right hand with the forefinger crooked and called down a blessing from heaven as her grandfather used to do. "Go gently," she whispered through the tears stinging her throat.

"Thankee, missus," Stewart's voice lingered after his image faded.

"Thank ye, Lizabet," Sarah's voice reached her as the portal closed and the oval of light incandesced and disappeared with a displacement of air that popped in her ears.

"Oh my." Elizabeth wiped tears from her cheeks. "It worked, didn't it?"

"It did indeed. Well done." Septimus clapped his hands.

"It was nicely done indeed," Gramma Lizzy concurred.

"And now, it is time for you to return to your office." Septimus smiled. "If we don't cross paths beforehand, I will see you when your time comes to take Lizzy's place."

"You mean when I die?" Elizabeth swallowed hard.

"In a manner of speaking, yes." He nodded.

"And you, Gramma Lizzy, you'll move on to the next plane when that happens?" Elizabeth looked to her great grandmother.

"I may, but I also think I will have the choice to stay and work with my great granddaughter, if I so choose. Time will tell. In the meantime, you have only to call me if you wish to visit. I look forward to Imbolc and hopefully speaking with Liza." Gramma Lizzy enfolded her in a hug.

"This is farewell for now." Septimus held out his hand.

"Until later, then." Elizabeth put her hand in his and squeezed, unwilling to say goodbye.

Septimus gave a stately half-bow and blinked out of sight.

Elizabeth stared at the spot where he disappeared for a long moment, reluctant to turn away.

"Come along, I'll take you back to your office and ensure that all is well before I leave you." Gramma Lizzy hooked her arm with Elizabeth's. "Don't forget to write everything you can remember down as soon as possible."

"I won't. I promise." Elizabeth leaned into the other woman for a moment. *How many people actually get to meet their great grandmother? How cool is this.*

The walk up to her office took far less time than Elizabeth would have liked. Each step taking her closer to the moment she would have to part with Lizzy.

"Here we are." Gramma Lizzy stopped by Elizabeth's office. "I think you'll find everything is in order." She cocked her head at the sound of voices and a heavy door shutting with a thud that echoed through the empty building. "I do believe that the world has begun to move forward again, and it is time for me to get back to work." Lizzy unhooked her arm from Elizabeth's and pushed open her office door.

Elizabeth hugged Lizzy, holding on as long as she dared.

"Go on, now." Lizzy stepped back and gave her a tiny push.

Time seemed to leap around her, Elizabeth's head spun and somehow she crossed the floor and sank into her chair. The chair that was already occupied, she noted, as her conscious mind melded with the body that had laid sleeping while she'd been haring off on the most bizarre and wonderful experience of her life.

Chapter Thirteen

"Oh, my goodness. Miss Warwick! Were you trapped here all night?"

The voice intruded on Elizabeth's sleep laden mind. Fighting her way through the pillowing waves of consciousness, she blinked and raised her head from the cradle of her crossed arms.

"Huh? What?" Forcing her eyes to open she focused on the bleary figure in her office door. "George? Is that you? What time is it?"

"Are you sure you're all right, Miss Warwick. Should I go and get someone?" The security guard hovered by her desk.

Elizabeth pushed herself upright and commanded herself to make sense of the situation. "Hi, George. Yeah, I was working late and by the time I realized how bad the storm was it was too late to try and get home. So, I just hunkered down here." She shook her head, belatedly realizing her hair was straggling over her shoulders. "I must have dozed off at some point."

"Good thing the backup generators kicked in or you'd be frozen stiff. There's donuts in the break room and I just made a fresh pot of coffee. You look like you could use some," George suggested.

"You are a saint." Elizabeth got to her feet, running her fingers through her hair in a vain attempt to tame it. "I'll just go along and drink about a gallon of it, right now."

"You do that." He smiled at her. "I'll just radio in that I've found you, safe and sound."

"Were people looking for me?" She paused on her way to the door.

"Yes. Your grandmother called my supervisor when you didn't show up at home and she couldn't reach you on your phone. She even checked with Winnipeg Transit just in case you were on one those buses that got marooned in the drifts and the passengers were evacuated to an emergency shelter."

Elizabeth whirled around and scrabbled under the paper strewn across her desk frantically searching for her phone. "Got it! I should have thought to call Gramma as soon as you woke me up. I'll do it now." Clutching the phone, she left the office in search of the aforementioned coffee.

She made her way through the echoing empty building to the break room. It must only be the security staff that had managed to make it into work so early. The scent of the caffeine laden brew drew her like a magnet. Minutes later, the largest mug she could find filled to the brim with sugary coffee, she settled at the round table by the snow encrusted window. It was a matter of seconds to call up her contacts and initiate the connection.

"Hello? Elizabeth, is that you?" Gramma answered on the first chirp of her phone.

"It's me. What a night." She took a huge drink of coffee.

"How was the night? I was frantic when I couldn't reach you after we spoke earlier. Did anything strange happen during the night..." Liza's voice trailed off expectantly.

"You could say that. Did you have any idea about the whole guardianship deal the female side of our family is supposed to be part of? Is that the reason we are expected to give one girl child a generation the name Elizabeth?" She drank more coffee and waited for Gramma to spill the beans.

"I know some of it. The stories that are passed down. It's just always been a family tradition to name one of your daughters Elizabeth," she replied.

"What if you only have one daughter and she's the first born and you call her something else? I mean, there's no way of knowing what the sex of a baby is before its conceived," Elizabeth pressed for more details.

"The only answer I can give you is the one my mother gave me. She said I would know when the child was born, that the name would come to me the moment I held her in my arms and looked into her eyes. Just as your mother, God rest her, knew when she bore you." Gramma Liza sniffed a little and Elizabeth heard her take of sip of something.

"Wasn't there something you could have shared with me and not let me go into this madness blindsided?" Elizabeth demanded.

"I'm not one of the chosen ones. I don't have any more information than you did before last night. The experience seems to skip generations, sometimes one, sometimes two. I suppose it depends on the lifespan of the participants..." Gramma speculated.

"You can be sure that I'm going to make sure my daughter, or daughters, and granddaughters know a lot more than *I* did beforehand," Elizabeth vowed.

"You must do what you feel is right. You are one of The Elizabeths and so your decisions will be the right ones," Gramma Liza assured her.

"What about tradition? Was it tradition that I should go into it without prior knowledge of what was going to be asked of me?" she demanded.

"Tradition is what tradition is. Like time, like society, traditions can change and mature. Perhaps, it is your calling to change how things have been done in the past," Gramma speculated.

"I suppose. Are you curious about what went on during the wee hours of the night?" Elizabeth teased, willing to change the subject from talk of tradition and her future children.

"Of course, I am. What can you tell me?" Gramma's voice vibrated with excitement.

"Well, I can tell you that I met your mother. My great grandmother Lizzy," she began.

"Really? How is that possible?"

"Your mother is one of the guardians. She is the original The Elizabeth, near as I can figure it. Before the legislature was built on that spot, the natives who lived here managed the whole light against dark thing in their own ways. But with the advent of the development in the area and the spread of the city, new methods were needed," Elizabeth explained as best she could.

"Hmm, I see. But why our family?" Gramma Liza mused.

"It's our heritage apparently. We're Warwicks by blood," Elizabeth said.

"What does that have to do with anything?" Liza sputtered. "None of our family worked on the building in its infancy."

"Maybe not. But one of the men who worked on the building as an architect was a Warwick. And he was a Master Mason from what I could gather. It was him and the other fellow who designed all the protections into the structure. The bison, the ox heads, Medusa and Athena. The rotunda and the Pool of the Black Star play a part too. That's why our family line is linked with the protections. It's in our blood, so to speak." Elizabeth drained her coffee cup and went in search of more. Filling her cup to the brim after adding three spoons of sugar. This was a conversation best leavened with caffeine.

"Well, I never..." Liza was astounded. "I wonder why Mother never told me?"

"I wish she'd told me," Elizabethe exclaimed, returning to her seat with coffee in-hand.

"I imagine she would have perhaps said something when you were older, but Mother passed when you were very young."

"True. Oh, by the way, Gramma Lizzy wants to see you—"

"What! How?"

"Hush and let me tell you. We thought that the best time would be one of the quarter or cross-quarter days when the veils between the worlds are thinner. We would need to be in the legislature building, either in the rotunda or by the Black Star. I thought maybe the summer solstice and if that didn't work we could try Samhain. What do you think?"

"I...I'm not sure. I'll have to think on that and find what day feels right to me. Perhaps the Tarot cards will help. Oh, that would be so wonderful to be able to see Mother one more time...." Liza's voice cracked on the last word.

"We'll do our best to see that happens," Elizabeth promised.

"Was it just you and Mother?" Gramma Liza asked.

"No, there was a man, he didn't look it, but I think he was much older than Gramma

Lizzy. He said his name was Septimus, I never heard his last name, if he even had one. And there were child spirits and oh, Lord, more things than I can talk about here. Tell you what, I'm going to see if I can get a ride home, call a taxi or something and I can explain it all to you when we're together," she promised.

"You'll never get a taxi in this mess. Most of the streets aren't even plowed yet. I'll call Frank, he's got a big Dodge four wheel drive that he uses out on the farm. It'll get through anything, and it has a blade on the front, so even if there's drifts he'll get through. I'm going to call him right now. Be ready and waiting by the main doors." The line went dead.

"Okay. I'll just security know I'm leaving..." Elizabeth laughed at the silent phone. Once Gramma got an idea in her head you might as well tell he wind to stop blowing as expect her to change her mind. She washed her cup in the sink and went along to her office to collect her outer clothes and her purse. There was no hurry, it would take Frank at least twenty minutes to cover the few blocks between home and here. After alerting George that she was vacating the building, she headed for the main entrance. Passing the library/reading room, as it was now known, she paused.

"Bye, Gramma Lizzy. Take care and see you soon," she whispered.

A slight movement of air caressed her cheek and then was gone.

Chapter Fourteen

"It's so good to be home." Elizabeth sank into the chair by the fireplace and accepted the cup of cocoa Gramma Liza handed her. "I feel like I could sleep for a week."

"Not before you tell me everything that happened last night, my girl." Liza took the chair beside her, setting a plate of chocolate cookies on the table between them.

"I'll do the best I can before falling asleep," Elizabeth promised, smothering a yawn. "I'm not sure even where to begin."

"Begin at the beginning, and go on until you come to the end, like Lewis Carroll says in Alice in Wonderland said. Or something close to that at any rate." Liza looked at her over the rim of her cup.

Elizabeth stared at the fire flickering in the Tyndall stone fireplace. Her favourite fossil was thrown into shadow by the flames. Gramma Liza nudged her with a toe, so she took a deep breath and began at the beginning.

* * *

"And then Gramma Lizzy walked with me back to my office, we said goodbye, and then I somehow morphed back into my...body...I guess is the only way I can describe it. Next thing I knew, George the security guard was at my door. Then I called you and went down to meet Frank. Where is Frank, by the way?" Elizabeth drank the last of her cooling cocoa.

"Frank's gone to pick up some groceries. He should be back anytime now. Why don't you go on up to bed and have a rest. You look ready to drop. I'll wake you when lunch is ready." Liza took the cup from her granddaughter's fingers.

"If you don't mind, that sounds wonderful. I feel like I've been dragged through a knothole backward, as Granddad used to say." Elizabeth got to her feet and moved toward the stairs.

Liza laughed. "Imagine you remembering that old saying." The crunch of heavy tires on packed snow interrupted her. "Oh, there's Frank now. I'll just go and help bring in the groceries and get them put away. You go up to bed, like a good girl."

Elizabeth smiled, the rejoinder bringing back happy memories of her childhood spent in this house after her parents died. Grasping the banister for support, she made her way up to her bedroom overlooking the large backyard with the tall oak trees arching over the gardens, reaching sturdy branches toward her window. A saucy squirrel chattered at her when she peered out the frosty pane.

"Sorry, buddy. I have to go buy some peanuts for you. We're all out," she told him.

When the window remained closed, the squirrel flicked his bushy black tail and scurried down the trunk in search of other sources of food.

"Silly thing." She grinned and flopped onto the bed, pulling the thick comforter over her, not bothering to undress. "Maybe I'll wake up and discover what happened last night was all just a dream, mostly a bad one at that." Elizabeth thumped the pillow once, rolled over and dropped into oblivion.

"Elizabeth! Supper!

Gramma Liza's voice penetrated the soft cocoon of sleep, forcing Elizabeth back into the land of the conscious. With more than a little reluctance, she struggled out of the warm shelter of her cover and put her feet on the floor. Rubbing the sleep out of her eyes, she caught sight of the digital clock on the dresser. "Oh my." How could it be 7 o'clock already? She padded over to the window where the night pushed against the panes. "I must have been more tired than I thought. I should have been helping with supper." Running a brush through her tangled hair, she shoved some combs in her hair, pulled her shirt straight and headed for the stairs.

"Coming, Gramma," she called, taking the steps two at a time like she used to as a child.

"There's no rush. Frank and I have everything in hand." Liza stuck her head out the kitchen door. "Eating in the kitchen tonight, it's cozy in here."

"Hey Frank," Elizabeth greeted the silver-haired man and slid into her spot at the table. "Thanks for helping Gramma. I meant to come down sooner but..." She shrugged.

"Understandable, after the night you've had. Liza has been telling me a bit about it while we got supper ready. Sounds like your Winter Solstice was a lot more exciting than ours." Frank shared a private look with Liza.

Elizabeth snorted and smothered a smile. "I bet your celebrations were a lot more romantic than mine."

"Yes, well." Liza turned to pick up a bowl from the counter to hide the blush staining her cheeks.

Giggling, Elizabeth got up and put her arms around Liza from behind. "I'm glad you had a nice night, Gramma. And I'm glad you had Frank to enjoy it with," she whispered. Giving her a last squeeze, Elizabeth picked up the bowl of vegetables and put it on the table.

"Ham, today as we'll be having turkey on Christmas Day," Frank said, putting a slice on Elizabeth's plate.

"And scalloped potatoes, my fav." Elizabeth took a generous spoonful and plopped it on her plate. For a few minutes the only sounds were cutlery on china and the odd request for more applesauce or salt.

Laying his fork down, Frank leaned forward on his elbows and arched his brows at Elizabeth. "Liza tells me you saw her mother last night, is that true?"

She swallowed the last bite of potatoes and nodded. "It is. Great Gramma Lizzy hangs out in the legislature reading room. She still refers to it as the library. It's kinda hard to believe the woman I met is actually my great grandmother."

"Why is that? Is there no family resemblance?" Frank wondered.

"It isn't that. But she's...well, she didn't look much older than me. Maybe in her late thirties or early forties?" Elizabeth replied.

"How strange. Mother was over ninety when she passed on," Liza mused.

"I kinda got the impression that the spirits could appear in whatever form they wanted." Elizabeth frowned. "Although the two young spirits seemed stuck in the form they were when they passed."

"You only mentioned the children in passing earlier. I suppose I was asking too many questions about Mother and that Septimus character. Where do the children fit in the picture?" Liza asked.

"I'm not sure they were meant to be part of the whole The Elizabeth against the Big

Bad thing. I know there's always been rumours about the security guards hearing kids in the basement, and the only name they've ever heard associated with the disembodied voices is Stewart. Whether that is the same Stewart as the spirit I met, I couldn't say," Elizabeth said.

"But they helped you, didn't they? Maybe they were supposed to be there," Liza reflected.

"Maybe. I don't know. They were both orphaned long before the building was constructed. Somehow, they're all tied to the place where they died, and none of them died easily. Maybe it's the remembered trauma that holds them there." Elizabeth shivered.

"Liza told me you helped the two of them move on. Is that so?" Frank's blue eyes crinkled. "How did you manage that?"

"I don't rightly know to be truthful. It was more helping them realize they could let go and go on."

"But how...?" Frank leaned forward; hands clasped tight on the table.

"It's not something I can explain. There are no words that can truly capture the experience. I suppose maybe that's the crux of the matter...you have to experience it to understand it. Oh, I don't know! I can't say as I actually understand it at all, but that's the closest I can come to telling you about it. There was a lot of bright light, and music...music like you've couldn't imagine...and spirits waiting for them on the other side…" Elizabeth's voice trailed off, her eyes gazing unseeing at the flame of the candle in the centre of the table.

"I can appreciate that, Elizabeth." Liza patted her hand and drew her attention from where it had wandered back to the supper table. "I've had experiences like that myself. When it's so extraordinary that mere words can't encompass the reality of what you've felt and experienced."

"Yes! That's exactly what it's like." Elizabeth gripped her grandmother's hand.

"Aye, I've had those experiences as well. It's just I always wonder if there were two people together when something like that occurs, do they both experience the same thing? Or do they experience something that is personal to them alone that is triggered by the same stimulus?" Frank nodded.

"Oh, you!" Liza tossed a bun at Frank. "You're always analyzing everything, when the most important thing is to have experienced it in the first place."

"If you say so, love." He smiled across the table at her.

Elizabeth grinned at them, then turned serious. "That's an interesting observation, Frank. I don't think there's really an answer for that though. I mean, how could you be certain that both parties were actually inspired by the same event, might they not be each inspired by a different aspect of the trigger?"

"Now, that's a very intriguing thought. You're saying that one event might actually have more than one component to it that would trigger different reactions in each person," Frank asked.

"Well, yes. For example, what if you and I were out at night and we came across a place where the veils are thin. In that place we both saw a shining figure with a horse beside them, a hare, and a fox at their feet. Now, what if, for me it takes me into a plane where the figure is mother figure and the horse is my transport to fairyland, or the land of the Sidhe. What would that image trigger in you?" Elizabeth proposed a scenario.

Frank frowned and closed his eyes. "I think for me, the figure would become a knight or a hero of some sort on a quest. There would be two horses, and the fox and hare are actually two great Irish Wolf Hounds." He opened his eyes and blinked. "Astounding! I believe you may be correct. A single event, or trigger, could manifest a whole plethora of experiences depending on the mindset of those encountering the trigger. How fascinating..." His voice trailed off, his eyes becoming unfocused.

"You're as bad as he is, Elizabeth. Don't encourage him." Liza tapped Elizabeth lightly on the arm and then snapped her fingers in front of Frank's nose. "Hey you, come back from wherever it is you've gone."

Frank blinked again and then smiled. "Sorry, love. But you know how I love a paradox."

"Sadly, I do." Liza shook her head. "Enough of this esoteric jibber jabber for the night. There's an old Christmas movie on in a few minutes and I want to watch it with my favourite people."

"That sounds great." Elizabeth gathered the dishes from the table and filled the dishwasher. Setting the pots and pans in the sink.

"You're actually going to use the dishwasher?" Liza teased her. "No comments about how lazy people have become, no wasting of water?"

"Not tonight." Elizabeth smiled over her shoulder. "It's Christmas, after all. And I've just survived the longest night of the year and come out the other side still smiling."

"Amen to that." Liza hugged her.

Epilogue

"I can't believe she's here." Elizabeth breathed hard through her nose and lay back on the pillows. "And on the night of the Winter Solstice..."

A tiny wail broke the silence in the room. She pushed herself up with her elbows and held out her arms. Her husband settled their new daughter in her arms. Elizabeth gathered the tiny bundle to her breast and smiled at Ian over the crown of red-gold hair that was all that was visible of new baby.

"Thank God she's here and you're both safe and sound." Ian wiped the sweat from his forehead with a washcloth. "You are okay, aren't you?" He laid a hand on her shoulder.

"As far as I can tell, I'm fine," Elizabeth assured him.

He moved to stand by the window, looking out into the storm that raged outside. Pulling the curtains closed against the draft, he turned back to his wife. "Trust you to decide to go into labour in the middle of a Winnipeg blizzard, and on the night of the Winter Solstice." Ian shook his head, but his smile took any sting out of the words.

"Just like me, for sure." She laughed and shared a private look with her grandmother who had just come into the room.

"Oh, I missed it," she exclaimed. "But then some things are best shared between husband and wife. Let me see the wee mite." Liza bent over the bed and put a gentle hand on the tiny head peeking out of the receiving blanket.

"Only just, Gramma," Elizabeth whispered.

"All is well?" Liza glanced at Elizabeth's belly and put clean towels on the bedspread.

"All good. Ian was a great coach, and we even managed not to destroy the sheets and mattress."

"No worry on that score. Things can always be replaced, people can't." Liza patted her arm. "Have you thought of a name for this little one?"

"She's my first born, and I want to carry on the tradition, so she's going to be Elizabeth Emily Warwick Worthington. We're going to call her Lilibet." Elizabeth reached out a hand to her husband. "Ian gets to name the next one, though."

"One is enough for now, love." His smile excluded everything except his wife and child. The blizzard raged outside, wind howling unheard down around the eaves. Liza slipped out of the room and went downstairs to report to Frank that all was right with the world.

The End

Nancy lives in Castor, Alberta with her husband and various critters. She is a member of the Writers Guild of Alberta and secretary of the Canadian Authors Association. Nancy has presented at the Surrey International Writers Conference, at the Writers Guild of Alberta Conference, When Words Collide and Word on the Lake. She has served as judge for the Writers Guild of Alberta – Alberta Literary Awards-YA Category. She has publishing credits in poetry, fiction, and non-fiction. Her work has been included in Tamaracks Canadian Poetry for the 21st Century, Vistas of the West Anthology of Poetry and The Beauty of Being Elsewhere. Her poetry is also being included by the University of Holguin Cuba in their Canada Cuba Literary Alliance (CCLA) program. The self-published Touchstone was reviewed in A Shower of Warm Light by Prof. Miguel Angel Olive Iglesius. Nancy is an avid horsewoman and a retired equestrian coach. She enjoys fostering rescue animals and gardening.

I have been a member of The Canadian Authors Association since August of 2021. Prior to that I was a member of The Writers Union of Canada for six years and often volunteered with them.

**_Nancy M Bell books also published
by BWL Publishing_**

Canadian Historical Brides Collection
His Brother's Bride ~ Ontario
Landmark Roses – writing as Marie Rafter
On A Stormy Primeval Shore with Diane
Scott Lewis

Canadian Historical Mysteries Collection
Discarded ~ Manitoba
The Tom Thomson Mystery ~ Ontario

The Cornwall Adventures
Laurel's Quest ~ Book One
A Step Beyond ~ Book Two
Go Gently ~ Book Three

The Alberta Adventures
Wild Horse Rescue ~ Book One
Dead Dogs Talk ~ Book Two
Chance's Way ~ Book Three
Laurel's Choice ~ A Laurel Rowan Story

Romance
Storm's Refuge A Longview Romance Book
One
Come Hell or High Water A Longview
Romance Book Two
A Longview Wedding A Longview Romance
Book Three
A Longview Christmas Seasonal Novella
Kayla's Cowboy A Longview Romance
The Selkie's Song ~ Book One

239

Arabella Dreams ~ Book Two

Historical Horror
By N.M. Bell
No Absolution

BWL Publishing

bwlpublishing.ca

www.ingramcontent.com/pod-product-compliance
Lightning Source LLC
Chambersburg PA
CBHW070012120726
47909CB00003B/899